On the third floor, I found the Prisoner Visitation Sign-In Room. The room, which could have easily been mistaken for a way station to hell, was packed with miserable souls — young women clutching scrawny toddlers with Kool-Aid stained faces, aging matrons with bad teeth and worn-out expressions, tired men wearing cheap vinyl jackets and chain-smoking Marlboro Lights. I sat at the remotest bench I could find, avoided eye contact with my desolate companions and waited for my name to be called. After the longest forty-five minutes of my life, I was led by a ghoulish-looking man who towered over me by at least a foot to the visiting area, a row of cubicles on the twelfth floor.

"Cubicle five," the deputy said. "You got fifteen minutes. I am required by law to advise you that all conversations are monitored."

I opened the door and found myself in a tiny room about the size of a phone booth. He sat on the other side of smeared glass reinforced with metal mesh. He looked pale, gaunt and frightened in his orange jail jumpsuit.

Seeing him again, the wild anger I felt yesterday nearly overtook me. I took a deep breath. I was here for a reason, I reminded myself. I needed to find out whether he was the killer . . .

Then Peter and the other apostles answered and said, We ought to obey God rather than men.

— *The Acts of the Apostles* 5:29

FINAL CUT

2 A CARMEN RAMIREZ MYSTERY

LISA HADDOCK

II

HADDO

THE NAIAD PRESS, INC.
1995

ISTKW

Printed in the United States of America on acid-free paper
First Edition

Edited by Christine Cassidy
Cover design by Bonnie Liss (Phoenix Graphics)
Typeset by Sandi Stancil

Library of Congress Cataloging-in-Publication Data

Haddock, Lisa, 1960 –
    Final cut / by Lisa Haddock
        p.   cm.
    ISBN 1-56280-088-4
    I. Title. II. Series: Haddock, Lisa, 1960 – Carmen Ramirez
mystery : 2/
PS3558.A31195F56   1995
813'.54—dc20   95-16170
                                                                    CIP

To Lisa Bell,
who always keeps life
interesting, entertaining, and exciting . . .

ACKNOWLEDGMENTS

The author wishes to thank: Mark Breithaupt, an investigator with the Rockland County, N.Y., Medical Examiner's Office, for information on crime scenes; my friend and Sooner expatriate Mark Stern, for information about Oklahoma City and Tulsa; and, as always, Lisa Bell, for invaluable criticism and insight.

ABOUT THE AUTHOR

Lisa Haddock was born and raised in Tulsa, Oklahoma. She holds bachelor's and master's degrees from the University of Tulsa. Like Carmen Ramirez, she is of Puerto Rican and Irish heritage. A journalist working in New Jersey, she lives with her life partner and cats.

AUTHOR'S NOTE

Frontier City, its institutions, and inhabitants exist only in the author's imagination. In particular, Frontier City University and its social organizations are a creation of the author's imagination.

CHAPTER ONE

Bending over me, the gunman shoved the gun in my face. I lay helpless, bound hand and foot, on the cold, hard ground. The barrel touched my nose. "This is how you kill somebody," he said to his accomplice.

"Noooooooooooo!" my friend Charles screamed.

The gunman's finger tightened around the trigger. Time slowed as if in a film advancing frame by frame.

I was twenty-seven and I was going to die at the hands of a mad man who had killed at least twice before.

1

If only I could have had another chance to see Grandma, to talk to her, to tell her I still loved her. She would never know. We'd fought terribly the last time we'd spoken, and that was months ago. My death would destroy her.

My father. He'd lost my mother when I was a baby. And now, he would lose me.

And my sweet, wonderful Julia. What would become of her? Who would take care of her?

"Dear God," I said inside my head, "please look after them."

It had all begun five months ago, in early September 1987. That time of the year in Oklahoma, it's still warm. The windows of my Honda Civic were rolled down when I pulled into the driveway of my garage apartment.

An angry, male voice pierced the late-summer night air. "We've got to be more organized, more visible. This is an all-out war for our survival."

It was twelve-forty-five. I saw the usual faces around the kitchen table. But they were joined by a newcomer. God in heaven, I nearly said aloud, it's Toni.

With a flicker of recognition in her eye, Antoinette Victoria Stewart, known to her friends as Toni, pulled a Marlboro from the pocket of her brown leather vest. We stared at each other for long moment. Her curly, light-brown hair had been much shorter the last time I'd seen her, more than four years ago. Now, she wore it loose and down to her shoulders. But she was still Toni. With tattered Levis, worn brown cowboy boots and sparkling, deep brown eyes, she made an impression.

"Carmen, how the fuck are you?" she said, resting her cigarette on the overflowing ashtray next to her. A sly, cool smile played across her face.

"Okay, Toni," I said, trying to keep my voice neutral.

Toni — charming and dangerous as ever — was sitting in my apartment. After more than four years, she still made my pulse quicken.

The owner of the loud, angry voice was Leonard Martin — a passionate young man with an overgrown goatee. His lank, long auburn hair was held back in a ponytail. Save for a green Mao cap, complete with red star, he was dressed all in black. "Look people," he said, continuing his diatribe, "it's nineteen eighty-seven. We've had Reagan since eighty-one, and we'll probably have someone just as bad after that. Homophobia is killing us. Silence is killing us. Indifference is killing us. The Reagan administration would be happy if we all die." Slapping our flimsy kitchen table for emphasis, Leonard sent my prized porcelain heifer salt-and-pepper shakers onto the floor. Oblivious, he lit up a Dunhill.

Leonard's outburst temporarily shook me from my thoughts of Toni. "Hi, folks," I said, looking around the kitchen of our small apartment. The place was a disaster — beer bottles, Coke cans, empty pizza boxes and paper plates were stacked on the counters, and the air was thick with cigarette smoke. Around the kitchen table were Julia Nichols, my lover and companion of two years, Donna Parker, a senior

3

theater major, Tom Gomez, a junior nursing student, and Leonard, a graduate English student. And, of course, Toni.

Beginning a few weeks ago, when the term started, Julia, a master's candidate in English at Frontier City University, and three of her fellow students had been working to launch a lesbian and gay student organization.

Their task would not be easy in Frontier City, Oklahoma, a city of 375,000 known for its religious fervor, political conservatism and oil wealth.

To be sure, Frontier City University — a small, private institution — was a haven in this Bible Belt stronghold. Still, it was not immune to the intolerance that pervaded the region. Though the faculty was liberal, the students were solidly right wing. Half were Oklahomans; most of the rest hailed from states of equally fundamentalist fanaticism — Arkansas, Texas, Missouri and Kansas. The sizable minority of foreign students stuck close to one another, keeping their heads down and their mouths shut.

I had expected the meeting to be finished by the time I came home from *The Frontier City Times,* where I worked as a copy editor.

I looked at Toni again. She smiled at me, her eyes bright and playful.

Julia cleared her throat. I glanced at her. She was clearly displeased. Shrugging my shoulders, I offered a weak smile.

"So," I said, turning away and looking back at Toni, "what are you up to?"

"First year of law school, babe. It's a real ass-kicker. I saw one of the fliers for this group around campus and I decided to show up. Weird or what?" she said, smiling without revealing any emotion.

"Yes," I said. "Very weird."

"Listen, kids," Julia said, "it's time for us to wrap up here. Next week, Tom, it's your turn to hold the meeting at your place. Am I right?"

"Julia, I still have the floor," Leonard said.

"Leonard, we always break it up by eleven-thirty. It's pushing one. And we still have to clean up," Julia said.

"Good night, everyone," I said, excusing myself. I headed to my bedroom and shut the door behind me.

Charles Dennis, my longtime friend, was stretched out on my bed with several books and my two cats: Wiley, a clever, inquisitive, lithe, gray kitty with white boots, and Holly, a placid, rotund butterscotch tabby with the personality of a Labrador retriever. A doctoral candidate in English in his fourth year at the University of California at Berkeley, Charles was staying with me and Julia while researching Cherokee folklore for his dissertation.

Wearing ripped gray sweat pants and a tattered Emerson High School Falcons swim team T-shirt, Charles looked up from his book — a treatise on linguistics. Six-foot-four and handsome with reddish-brown hair, greenish-blue eyes and a swarthy complexion, he was a mixture of Cherokee and French heritage. "Sorry to defile your boudoir with my masculinity, dear, but I had to escape that Eugene O'Neill drama playing out there in the kitchen."

"I thought she was out of my life for good," I said, sitting next to him on the bed and slipping off my black Converse All-Star high tops.

"Have you told Julia about her?"

I rubbed my forehead in dismay. Tell Julia? Yes, she knew the outline of my relationship with Toni. But how could I begin to tell her about the emotions this woman still stirred in me?

Toni and I met in a freshman philosophy class at Frontier City University. After that, I ran into her from time to time at events sponsored by the Progressive Students Coalition. Toni didn't care about the left-wing politics. She loved a good party, and she was too independent and tomboyish for the sorority scene.

At first, we were casual friends. Then Toni started phoning me. We could chat and giggle for hours about absolutely nothing. We hung out. Met every day for lunch. Shot pool. Went to basketball games. Drank beer. Talked about classes and soap operas and professors. Before I knew it, we were inseparable. Worse still, I developed a monster crush on Toni, who was involved — with a man. Making matters even unhealthier, I was deeply in the closet and frightened to death of my own desires. And Toni wasn't exactly the most supportive friend a young, sensitive, crushed-out closet dyke could wish for. She was moody, unreliable, self-centered and, above all, straight. But she was cool. God, was she cool. She could play softball like Reggie Jackson, ride horses as if she'd been born in the saddle, shoot pool like a pro (cigarette dangling from her lips all the while) and swear like a longshoreman. For three years, this ostensibly straight woman intrigued and fascinated me.

Everything fell apart during our senior year.

That's when I met Jane Swensen — a twenty-six-year-old graduate student in FCU's women's literature program — at a Progressive Students Coalition camping trip. I was instantly and overwhelmingly attracted to this outspoken, well-read, intelligent, radical woman — an open, obvious lesbian. From the first time I saw Jane, a short, sturdy woman with close-cropped sandy hair and lively blue eyes, I realized there was a lot more to love than a one-sided, sexless obsession for a straight woman.

I shamelessly hounded Jane for a date. She accepted. Quickly, we became lovers. I fell like the perennial ton of bricks. Staying in the closet seemed ludicrous. I came out to everyone in my circle of friends, including Toni.

I told Toni one night as we shot pool in the basement of her dormitory.

My words came out in a burst. "Toni, you probably already know this, but I'm a lesbian. I'm dating Jane, and I'm in love."

Pointing her pool cue, she surveyed the table. "Nine ball, corner pocket." Smoothly, she sank a complicated bank shot involving three rails.

"Aren't you going to say anything?"

"What's to say?" She sank another ball, this time with a combination shot to the side pocket.

"I don't know. How about, 'I accept you'? 'We're still friends'? 'I'm happy you're in love'? 'You have my blessing'? Any or all of those might do the trick."

"Hey, whatever makes you happy, babe," she said.

7

"Whoever you want to sleep with, well, that's none of my business."

I looked at her. Her face revealed no emotion.

"Are we going to shoot pool or what?" she said blankly.

I nodded at her, and she continued the game, not saying another word about me and Jane.

A few weeks later, I was working late one night at the college newspaper when Jane called.

"I don't know quite how to tell you this," she said grimly. "Your best friend was just here. She made a pass at me. I asked her to leave."

At first, I refused to believe it. I had to hear it from Toni. Giving myself a few days to calm down, I finally asked her to meet me at River Park. On a clear, cool spring day, I waited for her at a picnic table on the east bank of the murky Arkansas River. Across the river, I saw miles of oil refineries, vital to the city's economy yet disastrous for its environment. Long ago, these belching industrial monsters had made the river unusable for fishermen and swimmers. As always, the air was filled with a permanent sulfuric stench.

I didn't hear Toni walk up behind me. "What's doing, Carm?" she offered lightly.

Unable to speak for a moment, I looked up at her. She looked like the same, cool, charismatic Toni I had always known, in her jeans, T-shirt, cowboy boots and leather bomber jacket. Yet she looked uncharacteristically weary.

"Toni," I said, "I want to know why."

"Why what?" she said blankly as she sat across from me, her back to the river.

"I've been closer to you than I've ever been to

anyone else. I had so much fun with you for so long. We did so much together, and now that I have something really good going in my life, you try to ruin it."

She lit a cigarette and then looked at her fingernails. "I have no idea what you're talking about, Carmen." Her voice was without emotion.

"Jane said you made a pass at her."

"That's ridiculous," she said.

"Then she's lying? Toni, please tell me she's lying."

She shrugged and continued to study her fingernails.

"You won't deny it?" I hit the table with my fist. "You were my best friend. I trusted you. For God's sake, I took you to the hospital that night you had appendicitis."

"So?" she said with a shrug.

"What the hell are you talking about?" I shouted. "I would have given my life for you. You betrayed me."

"I betrayed you?" she said. "Join the club, babe. You ditched me first."

"Ditched you? How did I ditch you?" My heart froze. Could she have felt the same way about me?

"Open your eyes, Carmen. We were together practically twenty-four hours a day. That wasn't by accident."

My emotions were on overload. Toni — my idol, my hero — hadn't said that she loved me, but she may have felt a fraction of what I had felt for her. And then, reality set in. We had had three years together as buddies, and no more than that. And that whole time, she was dating somebody else.

9

"Toni, we were never a couple," I said. "You had a boyfriend. Remember? You're still going out with him. So why did you have to chase after my girlfriend?" Toni had been dating Bradley Pennington, a student at Southern Methodist University in Dallas, since they'd been students at the same suburban Oklahoma City high school.

"Jesus Christ, Carmen. Never a couple?" For the first time since I'd known her, I saw tears in her eyes. Even that night when she was doubled over from the appendicitis, she was stoic.

"What is it with you? You had three years to tell me how you felt," I said.

"You had the same three years."

"But you had a boyfriend."

"Big fucking deal," she said. She threw her cigarette on the ground and stamped it out with her cowboy boot. She looked me directly in the face, but her eyes were remote.

Staring at her, I felt the gulf between us. Just as grief was about to overwhelm me, anger took over. "I want an answer," I said. "Did you make a pass at Jane?"

"Let's say maybe I did. So what? We're like two people who went to a carnival together. We rode on all the rides, had a great time, and then, we got separated. And we could never find each other again. Nothing will ever change that now."

Tears streaming down my face, I walked off and hadn't spoken to her since.

Charles patted me on the back, shaking me from my memories. "What are you going to do?" he said.

"I don't know," I said, shaking my head.

"You want to talk about it?"

Charles had been there through the whole ordeal with Toni. He had seen me cry over her countless times. There was nothing more I could say to him.

"No," I said after a long while. "I don't want to think about it anymore. Let's change the subject. Tell me what's going on with you."

"Well," Charles said, "I locked horns with Leonard, that obnoxious, half-baked little twit. By the way, his Mao hat doesn't match the rest of his outfit."

I laughed. "What happened?"

Eager to tell a story, Charles put down his book and leaned forward. "I got home a couple of hours ago, happy as a potted plant. I'd just had a really productive session at FCU's Native American archives. So, I'm walking in, singing a tune from *South Pacific.*" Sounding a bit like a baritone Mary Martin, Charles started singing "I'm Gonna Wash That Man Right out of My Hair."

"Beautiful," I said. "Now get on with the story."

"All right," Charles said with a scowl. "I decided to sit in on Julia's meeting for a while."

"Sizing up the talent?" I said. I knew Charles well. He was forever on the lookout for a boyfriend.

"Oh, please," he said indignantly. "I got to talking with Leonard about my dissertation. And within a couple of minutes, he starts shrieking that I'm an 'academic Judas' because my dissertation isn't on a gay topic. Imagine the nerve. I'm out and proud every day of my life, honey. I don't need a lecture from him about it." Charles's voice rose with passion. "My Cherokee ancestors were marched here, torn from their homeland, thousands dying along the way. And I'm not allowed to study my own culture because it doesn't suit somebody I don't even know?" He was practically shouting.

"Did you say all this to him?" I asked.

"No," Charles said. "Do you think I should have?"

"It might have given him something to think about," I said. "But don't let him get you so upset. He's probably just trying to impress you. So, how's the research going?"

His face brightened. "The archives are helping a lot. The day after tomorrow, I'm heading out to the tribal headquarters in Tahlequah."

Charles was an ideal house guest, despite the crowded conditions in our one-bedroom apartment. Neat and considerate, he pitched in with the cooking, shopping and cleaning. He didn't complain about sleeping on the sofa bed, and he and Julia had bonded instantly, thanks to a shared love of books and the outdoors. Their raucous discussions and debates often lasted until the wee hours.

Charles continued, "I can't wait to start interviewing some of the older folks. I plan to videotape the sessions so I can really go over the nuances later — that is, if I can figure out how to use the camcorder."

"How's your Cherokee coming along?"

Charles rolled his eyes. "I have the vocabulary of a toddler right now."

Julia opened the bedroom door. As always, I

found her lovely. Wearing cutoff jeans and a FCU T-shirt, she was tall (five-eight to my five-six) and athletic with short blond hair. Her lustrous green eyes showed that she was less than happy.

"This is where I get off," Charles said. He picked up both cats and scooted out of the room.

"We've got a little problem here," Julia said when we were alone. "Leonard is crushed-out on Charles. Big time."

I was relieved she hadn't asked me about Toni. "Really?" I said.

"After the meeting, he poured his heart out to me. He thinks he may have ruined things by calling Charles an 'academic Judas.' "

"It's a unique pickup line," I said with a laugh. "Well, good luck to him. He certainly has gotten off on the wrong foot."

Dressed for bed and under the covers, I waited until Julia was brushing her teeth to tell her the big news. "By the way, did you know that was Toni Stewart?" I said.

"Yeah, I know." She continued brushing her teeth. "I saw the way you looked at each other."

"If you knew she was coming, why didn't you say anything?" I said as she came back into the bedroom.

After putting on an oversized Mickey Mouse T-shirt that made her look even younger than her twenty-two years (she was nearly twenty-three), she crawled into bed beside me.

"I didn't know it was the same Toni. Tonight was the first time I ever saw her. She responded to one of the fliers yesterday, called for directions to the meeting, and that was that. She just told me her first name and that she was a first-year law student. She didn't say two words until you came in."

"It certainly was strange seeing her again," I said, trying to sound casual.

"Not that it's any of my business, but —"

"Julia, I've told you before. We never slept together. We weren't lovers. I was infatuated with her, but that was years ago. It's over." As I said the words, I hoped they were true.

Julia's face remained troubled. "I didn't mean to grill you about this. Your past is your past."

"Please don't worry about it."

Turning her back to me, Julia settled into bed. She was quiet for a long time. I turned out the light and lay down beside her, my chest against her back.

"She's cute," Julia said.

"If anything, I should worry. She goes after my girlfriends, not me." I tried to chuckle, but it sounded false.

When Julia was asleep, I rolled away from her and thought about Toni. Memories of her would drift into my mind when I heard a song she liked on the radio (usually some mindless, head-banging heavy metal), when I drove past one of our favorite bars or pizza parlors, or when I would hear someone use one of her favorite vulgar expressions, like "fuckin' A, man." But now, she was powerfully back in my consciousness. She still exuded the same rough sexual energy that had captivated me years ago. Only now I wasn't shy, closeted and inexperienced. Now I could meet her on an equal footing. The attraction was still there, and if I made a move, she might well respond.

And then, at last, I would know what it was like to be with her.

I sighed. How could I think this way when the woman I loved was sleeping next to me?

The following afternoon, I was drinking coffee at the kitchen table and reading the newspaper when Charles came into the living room. Reeking of Calvin Klein Obsession for Men, he was dressed a white long-sleeve, button-down shirt and black slacks, both immaculately starched and pressed. His thick, shaggy, reddish-brown hair was pulled back in a ponytail. He wore two small silver hoop earrings, one in each ear.

"You look gorgeous. And you smell even better. What's the occasion?" I said.

"Thank you, love," he said, bowing slightly. "I'm heading to the library. I've got my eye on this cute little grad student who's been hanging out in the archives. Do you think a tie would be too much?" He held out a large silver and turquoise bolo tie and straight black tie for my inspection.

"No tie," I said.

"How do my shoes look?" He lifted up his pants legs to reveal his black penny loafers, which were polished to a high sheen.

"The glare is blinding. They're fine," I said. "Besides, don't fall in love yet. You have another admirer."

"Really? Who?" Charles said, clapping his hands like a schoolboy.

"Somebody from Julia's group."

"Tom Gomez? He seems sweet."

"No. Leonard."

"Eeeeyeeeuw," he said. "Please say you're kidding."

"No. Not at all. He told Julia he's sweet on you."

Charles gave me a tragic look. "Oh no. Why him? Dear God, why me?"

"He's not bad looking," I said.

"I don't judge a man exclusively by his looks, Carmen. Well . . . except for Tom Cruise. I'd be his sex slave in a heartbeat."

"You're always saying you want a relationship. Leonard seems nice enough."

Putting his hands on his hips, Charles regarded me with irritation. "He's pushy and annoying, he talks too loud, and he'd want to pick out a china pattern and wall sconces on the second date. I can't even have an academic debate without wanting to strangle him. And you want me to marry him?"

"Okay. I'm convinced," I said, holding up my hands in surrender.

Late Friday morning, clad in my grubbiest gray sweat pants and sweat shirt, I sat sipping coffee. I had the house to myself. Julia was in class and Charles had gone to the library to woo the latest object of his affection. I had half an hour to kill before I headed to the bowling alley to roll four or five practice games. I had never been an athlete and was only a mediocre bowler (my best game was maybe 160, and that was when I was bowling out of my head). Back in July, I tried out for a league sponsored by Crystal's Tavern, the only women's bar in town. I hadn't made the cut, but Crystal assured me that if I kept working on my game, they'd try to make a place for me in the winter league.

I had just put on Streisand's *The Broadway Album* — Barbra's finest work in years — when the phone rang.

"Is Charles in?" said a nervous, eager voice that was so loud I had to hold the phone away from my ear.

"Leonard?" I said.

He paused. "Carmen?"

He *was* obsessed, the poor devil. "Yes, it's Carmen. Leonard, he's out at the moment. May I take a message?"

"Do you know whether he's seeing anybody?"

What is this, I thought, seventh grade? "He's not into anything serious right now because of his graduate work. He'll be heading back to California in a few months."

"Do you think he might like me?"

Oh shit, I thought. "We haven't discussed it."

"I want to ask him out. Did I offend him really badly? He seemed really pissed off. I didn't realize he was an Indian — I mean Native American — until Julia told me."

Poor guy. He was trying very hard. "I'll deliver your message, Leonard," I said patiently. But I realized I was growing more irritated by the minute because I had started shredding Kleenex one by one. Charles was right. There *was* something grating about Leonard — he was clumsy, clingy, overbearing, like a Labrador leaping on you and demanding attention. On a dog, it was endearing. On a person, it was downright weird.

"Do you think he'll go out with me? I'm mean, he's a really nice guy and all. Does he date white guys? I would totally understand if it's a racial issue."

Charles dated men every color of the rainbow. But I didn't tell Leonard that. Their problem was chemistry, not skin color. "You'll just have to see how things work out."

"Well, at least tell Charles I'm really sorry."

"Want some friendly advice?" I said. "Stop beating yourself up over this."

"You're right," he said, sounding miserable. "Just tell him I called. I'm in the book. I'm the Leonard Martin with the FCU address. Please don't forget."

As soon as I hung up, I looked up and saw Toni, standing in my doorway and smiling her cool smile.

"Hi, Toni," I said casually, despite my increased pulse rate. "How long have you been standing there?" I opened the door and ushered her in.

"Not long. Cool digs, babe," she said as she surveyed my small living room, decorated in Kmart specials, thrift store acquisitions and my grandmother's castoffs. Toni came from money, though she always came across as a blue-collar tomboy. The only conspicuous signs of wealth she allowed herself were expensive watches and expensive cars. Today, she was wearing a Rolex and driving a showroom-fresh red BMW sports coupe.

"Thanks," I said.

"I was just eavesdropping on your conversation, Carm. You really shouldn't leave your windows open. So who's hot for Charles?"

Toni's fondness for hearing about the misery of others was one of her least appealing traits.

I didn't answer.

"It was that geek Leonard, wasn't it? Oh come on, Carmen. He was all over Charles at the meeting. He's about as subtle as a neon sign. Loser."

"Why is somebody a loser just because he or she feels deeply for somebody who can't or won't reciprocate?" We both knew I wasn't just talking about Leonard.

She smiled at me. She knew how to break the spell of an intense moment. "He's not important enough to argue about. Chill out, babe." She plunked herself down on the sofa and propped her cowboy boots on the coffee table. She unbuttoned her leather vest to reveal a ripped white T-shirt. Slim, tall and small-breasted, Toni usually went braless. Today was no exception. Lighting a cigarette, she said, "Where the fuck are your ashtrays? Don't you smoke anymore?"

"I haven't smoked for years. Let me find you one."

"So you're still listening to Streisand?" she said as I returned from the kitchen with an ashtray.

"She's one of the constants in my life. Somebody I can count on."

Toni ignored the gibe.

"Listen, I'd love to have you hang out, but I'm heading out to the bowling alley in a few minutes."

"Mind if I tag along?"

I was easily intimidated. Toni, a superb athlete, would be hard to bowl in front of.

"All I'm doing is practicing."

Toni smirked. "Are you in a league, babe?"

I shook my head and blushed. "Just practicing. You're not a good bowler, are you?"

"Nah, don't worry. It's been years since I've even been near an alley."

I ran into the bedroom and slipped into a pair of Levis and a T-shirt advertising the Frontier City Roughnecks, our local Double A baseball team. I grabbed my bowling bag and we headed off to Rose Lanes.

After the seniors leagues cleared out, Rose Lanes was nearly abandoned. Dot — a woman in her fifties with drawn-on eyebrows and a large, coal-black bouffant highlighted by a white triangular patch radiating from the middle of her forehead — ran the front desk during the day. She waved and smiled as I approached.

"Why howdy, Carmen."

"Can I have my usual two lanes?" I asked.

"Sure thing, hon," she said. "Does your friend here need shoes?"

Toni smirked. "Sure thing," she said, mocking Dot's thick Mississippi accent. "Size nine, if you please."

As we walked to our assigned lanes, I scolded

Toni. "I come here all the time. Did you have to sneer her? She's very nice."

"I don't befriend everyone the way you do, Carmen. Besides, she didn't know I was making fun of her."

"How do you know that?"

"Okay, I'm sorry," Toni said with a shrug. "I was cruel. I mocked her to amuse you. You used to like it when I did accents. You want me to go back and apologize?"

"Of course not. Then she'll know for sure you were making fun of her."

I sat down at the desk in front of our lanes.

"I forget. How heavy a ball should I get?" she asked.

Good, I thought. She didn't even know what kind of ball to use. Maybe that would mean I would have a chance to impress her. "Twelve pounds or more. Take the biggest you can handle comfortably."

Toni returned with two balls — one black, the other red.

"I just couldn't decide on a color. Any tips?" she said, smiling. She was definitely going all out to charm me. And it was working.

"Roll the ball as smoothly as possible, just to get an idea of how it's going to break on you. We can fine-tune your game from there."

"Thanks, coach." Winking at me, she peeled off her vest. Then she strolled over to the ball return and made an elaborate show of drying off her right hand over the air jet, just the way the pros do on television.

"Anytime today would be fine," I said, pretending her antics did not entertain me. "The leagues take over again in about five hours."

"Don't get your panties in a knot," she said, positioning herself at the very end of the lane.

After flawless approach, she slid just short of the foul line and released the ball with grace and power. Hooking perfectly into the pocket, the ball produced a solid strike.

I could have worked for years and never had a delivery like that. Clearly, Toni wouldn't be impressed by anything I could do. "How long has it been since you bowled?" I said.

"At least ten years."

For the next hour and a half, I watched in amazement as Toni, always at her best while showing off her athletic prowess, beat me soundly five games in a row. I was back where I was years ago. Once again I was Toni's adoring cheerleader, and she was the confident jock. The position was comfortable, familiar and intolerable.

"So I gather you're with Julia?" Toni asked as we drank iced tea with fresh mint from my garden after our session at the alley.

Without the distraction of bowling, I was more nervous than ever around Toni. Fear, anger, attraction and admiration were each vying for dominance inside me. "We've been together two years," I said as I sat in the rocking chair across from Toni, who was on the couch.

"So, you're like married or what?"

"Yes, very much so."

"She seems nice."

I studied her face. Her deep brown eyes squinted slightly as her mouth offered a smirk. Was she being playful or cruel? Was she disappointed that I wasn't single? Yes, I wanted her to be disappointed.

"How's the old lady?" she said, referring to my grandmother, Edna Sullivan, who had raised me.

"Her health is good, thank God. She's steaming right along."

Leaning back, Toni stretched up her arms then laced her fingers behind her head. "Does she still hate my guts?"

"You can't really blame her," I said, trying to ignore the way the pose highlighted her breasts. "The first time she ever met you, you had just gotten me very stoned on some high-octane pot."

"You wanted to try it, Carmen."

I had smoked marijuana a handful of times, all with Toni. I hated the way it made me feel — disoriented, dazed and helpless, as if trapped in a world where time stood still. "She always preferred to think that you had corrupted me. Anyway, she hasn't mentioned you in a while."

"That's good. At least I don't have to worry about those death threats anymore." She laughed. Much to my relief, she lowered her arms, folding them in her lap.

"You're not still into that mess, are you?" I said.

"Oh please, not in years. How many times can you get loaded and listen to Iron Butterfly? Besides, with law school, how could I manage?"

We didn't talk for a while.

"So how come Jane's no longer in the picture?" Toni asked.

For a moment, I couldn't answer. The memory of Toni trying to sleep with Jane was too painful.

"I hope I'm not out of line."

I took a deep breath to compose myself. "She got back together with her ex."

"After you moved to St. Louis with her?"

"Yes. I was heartbroken. It nearly destroyed me." Just like Toni nearly did, I reminded myself.

She paused. "You still talk to her?"

"We send each other cards now and then. Why, do you want her number? She's still with Rita, but that sort of thing doesn't slow you down, does it?" I said, my bitterness escaping suddenly.

"Are you fucking crazy?" she said, cutting off my anger with a mocking look.

There was a long, uncomfortable silence.

"So how are your folks?" I asked, trying to sound pleasant again. Mr. Stewart was a high-ranking executive at the state's largest bank — SoonerBank Inc.; Mrs. Stewart was a housewife. Both parents had inherited substantial wealth — Mr. Stewart from his father, a wildcatter in the oil fields; Mrs. Stewart from her family's sprawling western Oklahoma cattle ranch.

The question seemed to make her uncomfortable. "They're okay," she said, folding her arms across her chest.

"I guess they're really proud and excited about your going to law school."

"I suppose." Her tone was noncommittal.

"How's your brother?"

At this question, her face brightened and she relaxed. Back when Toni and I were friends, her brother, Paul, had been a bratty, sullen teen. But despite her hardness and cynicism about most of life, Toni dearly loved her brother.

"He's in his sophomore year at FCU now. He's a bigtime frat boy-business major — just like Dad," she said.

"What have you been doing between graduation and now?"

"A little of everything. I worked for my dad at SoonerBank. Then I went out to San Francisco for a while. I was there about ten months. It was great. There were eight of us living in a four-bedroom Victorian." She smiled at the memory.

"Why did you leave?"

"You know. Things like that tend to be really unstable," she said. "And it was time to buckle down and go to law school. I came back this spring." She looked wistful.

"You still seeing Bradley?"

"Well, yes," she said, seeming ashamed of her answer.

"What's the story on you two?"

She reached up and ran her hand through her light brown curls. "He's in law school, too. Third year."

"At FCU?"

She nodded, still tugging at her hair.

"Are you going to marry him?"

Her face grew troubled. "How should I know?" she said.

"You've been dating him about a hundred years. It seems like a natural question."

She said nothing.

"Does he know you're involved in this gay and lesbian group?"

Again, she said nothing, but I wouldn't back off. "Does your involvement mean that you're ready to come out?"

A neutral expression returned to her face. "I feel the way I do about people, and that's that. Why does it require some sort of label?"

"And how did you feel about me?" I couldn't believe I had asked her.

"I felt. . . . Look, I don't want to go over this again. We're here now. We're both a lot older. Why revisit the old stuff?"

"Because it's never been resolved."

Looking annoyed, she stood up and put her hands on her hips. "Carmen, we had a great day. Does it have to end like this?"

Toni had always fled from her feelings, but this time I wasn't going to let her get away. "I think you owe me an answer," I said.

"You want an answer? I'll give you one, babe," she said, calmly issuing a challenge. "I've got a town house right across from FCU. Come by any day for lunch. We'll spend the afternoon together — just you and me. We'll do anything you want. Just call me when you're ready."

"You mean it?" I said.

"Yeah, if you think you can handle it," she said seductively as she walked over to the chair where I was sitting. She put her hands on my shoulders and pushed me back in the chair. Then, she gave me a long sensual kiss on the mouth.

I was intrigued, yet too cautious to respond.

"Gotta run, babe," she said, pulling away. "I have a class. Don't forget to call." With that, she breezed out the door.

Toni dominated my thoughts for the rest of that Friday. I found myself thinking of that kiss, daydreaming about her smile, picturing how she moved and imagining our afternoon together, with us winding up in bed. Saturday, the spell still hadn't worn off. I hoped Julia was too busy with her studies to notice my distracted state.

Sunday and Monday were my regular days off. All day Sunday, Julia and Charles were in the way, trying to involve me in their conversations and activities. Monday morning, I waited until they left the house. Then I made my move. My heart pounded as I dialed Toni's number.

"Nothing serious is going on here," I told myself. "I'm only calling an old friend to arrange a nice, quiet lunch."

Toni and I arranged to meet the following Monday. Julia and Charles would be busy, and we would have the whole day to ourselves.

When I hung up, I was trembling.

CHAPTER TWO

The phone woke me from a deep sleep.

"Why aren't you here yet?" Grandma demanded.

Edna Sullivan, my grandmother, was the only mother I had ever known. She had taken over my care when I was one, just after my mother died.

"What?" I looked at my clock. It was noon Wednesday. I had overslept. I was supposed to be at Grandma's house for lunch at eleven-thirty. "Oh, I'm sorry. I was asleep. I'll be right over."

I hurriedly dressed and headed for the front door. Charles, wearing a dark suit because he was presenting a paper that afternoon at FCU, was eating lunch at the kitchen table.

"I'm late for lunch with Grandma."

"Plead the Fifth," he said.

I raced over to Grandma's home, about a mile away. Grandma lived in a small white frame house with a screened-in porch in a working-class neighborhood in the center of the city. She and my grandfather Clyde had moved there as newlyweds back in the thirties.

Grandma, her long white hair held back in a single braid, was standing in the yard. Dressed in a green and white floral housecoat and a hand-knitted beige sweater, she was weeding one of her flower beds as I drove up. Her late-summer garden was going strong, producing roses, chrysanthemums, zinnias and impatiens.

"I'm really sorry," I said, running up to her.

Grandma paused. "Brother Rex did a sermon on sleep last Sunday. You can't fall asleep at a normal hour and then you sleep late — because of that . . . lifestyle of yours." She spat out the word *lifestyle* with contempt.

A staunch Southern Baptist, Grandma and I had maintained a uneasy, brooding truce for more than a year on the issue of my "lifestyle." I thought that, finally, my seventy-one-year-old grandmother had accepted the fact that I was a lesbian and an ex-Baptist.

It had been at least a year since she had tearfully begged me to return to the church, which I had left at age seventeen.

Grandma had calmed down considerably on the subject of Julia. At first, she had vehemently objected to our relationship. Six month later, she had settled into silence. She didn't accept our involvement, and Julia was not welcome in her home, but she could talk to me without calling down the wrath of God.

Clearly, Charles's arrival that summer set the old girl off again, although she had yet to say anything direct about it.

His presence in our household had had a similar effect on the rest of the family. A couple of years back, I had told my father, Raúl Ramirez, who lived in New York City, about Julia, but he chose to ignore our relationship. His brain was wired exclusively for heterosexuality. When Charles arrived, Raúl was convinced that both Julia and I would wind up pregnant.

Julia's parents, Bob and Naomi Nichols of Wilton, Arkansas, had warmed up to being stiffly polite to me after the first year. Two women and a man not related by blood living in the same house had stunned them. They retreated to their Bibles to pray over the matter.

"Do we have to go through this again?" I said. "You know we get along much better when we don't have this discussion."

Grandma shook her head to ward off my comment. "The Bible says the wicked 'sleep not, except they have done mischief; and their sleep is taken away, unless they cause *some* to fall.' "

"I work the night shift. I wasn't out doing mischief, for God's sake."

"Don't you dare blaspheme the name of the Lord or his holy Word, girlie."

I shrugged. "Sorry. Look, I don't want to fight with you."

"Do you know what the Bible says about your kind of living?"

After seventeen years in the Baptist Church, it was a cinch that I would be familiar with whatever Scripture she was going to hurl at me.

"In Romans, Chapter One, the Apostle Paul says that women who burn in lust one toward another are worthy of death. And in Proverbs, it says, 'There is a way which seemeth right unto a man' —"

" 'But the end thereof are the ways of death,' " I interrupted.

I had been Scripture memorization champion three years running at my Sunday school. In my prime, I could spit out verses like a machine gun, outquoting even Grandma. But I had been away from the church nearly ten years, and time had eroded some of my prowess.

" 'The Lord said, My Spirit shall not always strive with man,' " Grandma hissed. "And you're fixing to cross that line. There's no return."

"Are you finished?" I said with a sigh.

Grandma glowered at me, then gave up. "You might as well come in. There's soup on the stove, but I've got to reheat it."

I followed her into the house. She had set a neat table, with a fresh pink rose in a vase sitting on a gleaming white tablecloth. "Grandma, the table is lovely," I said. "You shouldn't have gone to all this trouble."

She ignored my compliment as she set out a plate of cold cuts and rolls in front of me. "I got those whole-wheat deli rolls you like."

"Thank you. That was very sweet of you," I said.

"By the way, Mrs. Harmon, that lady from my

Sunday school class, said she saw a fancy red BMW parked in front of your house the other day. I told her she had to be mistaken." Grandma stared at me.

Grandma's Baptist churchwomen's gossip network rivaled the KGB. "No. She was right," I said. "That was Toni Stewart's car."

As soon as I saw the furious look on Grandma's face, I regretted being honest with her.

"That reprobate!" Grandma said angrily. "What in hell is she doing around here?"

"She's going to law school at FCU."

"Just what the world needs — a dope-smoking lawyer. She still hooked on that weed?"

I didn't answer her.

Grandma looked at me sternly. "What did she want from you?"

"Oh, we were just catching up on old times." Despite Grandma's looming, disapproving presence, I couldn't help but smile when I thought about Toni, about what was going to happen between us Monday, just a few days from now.

"Just look at you," Grandma said in utter disgust.

Grandma had once reacted similarly when she caught me watching the video "Like a Virgin" on MTV. She walked in just as I was ogling a scantily clad Madonna roll around on the streets of Venice.

"You stay clear of her. She's trouble."

I said nothing.

"Do you hear me?" she demanded.

"Yes, ma'am, I hear you," I answered. She was right. Toni was trouble. But I wasn't going to admit that to her. "Despite what you and your spy Mrs.

Harmon think, I'm no longer a minor. I'm twenty-six years old. I'll be twenty-seven soon. I make my own decisions, including who my friends are."

She glared at me. "Have some chips. I'll get the soup."

I left the bag of Fritos unopened while I waited for her to come back.

"Is Charles one of those fairy boys?" she said as she put a bowl of vegetable soup in front of me.

Sometimes, she could push me so far that I wanted to scream. "He's gay, Grandma," I said, struggling to control myself, "not a fairy."

Grandma's expression grew fearful. "Do you want to wind up with AIDS, having that man in your house?"

I rubbed my face in exasperation. My head was throbbing. "Charles is welcome in my home regardless of his HIV status. You can't catch HIV by having someone in your house."

"So he has it?"

As of his last test, he was negative, but I refused to cater to her hysteria. "That's none of your business."

She folded her arms over her chest and squinted at me. "Well, answer me this. Why did God send the ten plagues on Egypt?"

I didn't reply.

"Because Pharaoh hardened his heart," she said.

"Grandma, the Scriptures say that *God* hardened Pharaoh's heart. It seems to me that Pharaoh didn't have any choice in the matter."

"Don't you play word games with me, girlie," she

said, wagging her finger at me. "You think you have the Bible all figured out, don't you? Well you don't. Jesus said, 'By your fruits ye shall know them.' And what is the fruit of homosexuality?"

I didn't respond.

"The Bible says clearly, 'The wages of sin is death.' AIDS is the punishment from a just, righteous God for the sin of homosexuality."

"That's it," I said. I got up from the dining room table and stood in the living room.

"You're walking out?"

"I absolutely cannot listen to this anymore."

The old woman started to cry. "Don't you even care about me?"

I looked around the living room. Her gold, crushed-velvet recliner sat in front of her beloved television. Between them was a coffee table, with the latest *TV Guide* and several religious magazines fanned out for any visitor's perusal. Her well-worn, black leather-bound Bible sat at the center of the table. In this house, where she had lived for more than fifty years, that Bible had helped her survive the tragic, untimely deaths of her two children and her husband. The first to go was her son, Buster, killed in a hunting accident while still in his teens. Next, a heart attack felled my grandfather. He passed away a few months after my mother married my father. Grandma always said the shock of his fair-haired daughter's marriage to a "low-down Porta-Rican" killed my grandfather. Shortly after moving to New York City with my father, my mother was killed in a car accident. My father, committed to running a travel agency with his brother, sent me back to Oklahoma to be raised by Grandma. I looked at the mantel over her false fireplace. It was adorned with pictures of my dead mother, uncle and grand-father — and me. Above was a large framed painting of Christ, praying in agony in the Garden of Gethsemane. That Bible and I were all she had in the world.

"Of course I care," I said, patting her arm to reassure her. "But I can't stay if you don't respect me, Grandma."

She shook her head and sobbed, burying her face in her apron. "I'm an old woman, Carmen. I do the best I can. I can't give up on you and consign you to hell."

I gave her a stern look. "I will never, ever go back to the Baptist Church. You have the right to believe that way you do. And I have that same right."

She looked at me with dismay, the anxiety on her face making her look frail to me for the first time in my life.

After a silent, strained lunch, I went home.

As the days passed, my obsession with Toni grew into a frenzy. All I could think about was her, that kiss, and what was going to happen on our lunch date.

Sunday afternoon, the day before our lunch, I was alone in the house. Julia and Charles had asked me to go hiking with them, but I had encouraged them to go without me. I needed the time to fantasize about Toni.

A knock at the door stirred me from my

thoughts. Grandma, dressed in her Sunday best blue-and-white flowered polyester frock, stood at the door. In the two years Julia and I had lived here, she had never stopped by, despite numerous invitations.

"Grandma, what a surprise." I smiled, happy that she had finally come by for a visit, and opened the door. "Is everything okay?"

She nodded. "Where are your . . . friends?" She said *friends* as if it were a curse word in a foreign language.

"They're hiking," I said.

"Lord, I hope they don't run into any rattlers," she said as she looked over the small living room, which, luckily, had been recently cleaned up.

"Can I get you some coffee or a Coke or a sandwich or something?"

"Coffee if it's already made. Otherwise, just a Coke. I had lunch up at the Kentucky Fried Chicken right after church. Brother Rex presented a powerful sermon today," she said.

"That's nice," I said, hoping she wouldn't summarize the sermon's high points. I went to the kitchen to grind beans for a fresh pot of coffee.

"I told you I only wanted it if it was already made. All that clatter sounds like the end of the world."

"So what brings you here?" I said as I brought her a mug of coffee. She had sat in the rocking chair across from the sofa.

"Oh Lord, help me, that coffee looks strong," she said, her expression sour.

I sat down on the sofa across from her.

"I have to talk to you, Carmen," she said, giving me a piercing stare with her blue eyes.

"Yes," I said. "Go on." My blood ran cold. Whatever she was going to say, it wouldn't be pleasant.

"Are you having troubles . . . with your lady friend?"

"What?" I was stunned.

"If you're not getting along —"

"I am. I mean, we are."

"Clyde and I were together twenty-five years. Back then, marriage was for life. These days, seems like the world tells you, 'If you get an itch in your drawers for whatever happens down the road, you just follow it.' I raised you better than that, didn't I?"

Damn, was the old woman psychic? *One little kiss from Toni. That's all it was. And I didn't even initiate it.*

Grandma gave me another long stare. " 'For out of the heart proceed evil thoughts, murders, adulteries, fornications, thefts, false witness, blasphemies.' " Grandma stood up. "Well, I've said what I have to say."

And with that, she left.

Hot and dirty from their hike, Julia and Charles returned early that evening.

"Dibs on the shower," Charles said, running to the bathroom.

"What did you do today?" Julia said when we

37

were alone. She sat down beside me on the couch and kissed me on the ear.

"Oh, I just futzed around the house. You know, Grandma stopped by."

"That's weird. What was the occasion?"

"She just wanted to chat."

"Your grandmother came to this den of iniquity on the Sabbath for the first time in two years just to chat? Sounds awful fishy to me."

"Oh, it was nothing," I said. "Just something about her will."

Julia gave me a playful squeeze on the thigh and whispered in my ear, "Hey, Charles is going out tonight to be a bar-hopping tramp. You want to fool around?"

Guilty about my lies and my growing desire for Toni, I felt a strange distance between me and Julia. "Oh, I don't know."

"Oh, come on Carmen. We're practically still on our honeymoon. We're supposed to make out like crazed ocelots every chance we get."

"I'm sorry, baby," I said. "This ocelot just ain't in the mood."

Monday morning, Julia and I ate breakfast in silence. I got up early to make her French toast, which she loved. Charles had left hours earlier to drive to the University of Oklahoma in Norman, where he was presenting a paper.

"So," Julia said, "what are you going to do today?"

I hesitated. Should tell her about my lunch date

with Toni? If it's really nothing, I told myself, there's no reason she shouldn't know about it. "I've got to do some grocery shopping, and it's my turn to clean the bathroom."

"Carmen, is everything still okay between us?" Julia said, her face filled with worry.

"Yes, of course it is," I said. *God, what am I doing?* "You know how I feel about you."

"I thought I did, until Toni showed up in our living room two weeks ago. Ever since then, you've been distant. Every time I touch you, you move away."

Julia noticed. Grandma noticed. Everybody in town probably knew by now. "Toni?" I said. "She's just an old friend." And a full-blown obsession.

"Carmen, you're the one person in the world I can always count on. I hate feeling like this — jealous, possessive, worried. Tell me I'm just being silly." She nervously ran her hand through her short blond hair.

"You're just being silly," I said quickly. I hated myself for the ease with which I lied.

That afternoon, I got ready for my date with Toni. After I had taken a long bath and splashed myself with Opium, I combed back my straight, black hair, which I kept short on the sides, a bit longer on top. I put on my fancy black lace bra and panties, my black jeans, a black tank top, a black Western shirt with white pearl-front snaps and black cowboy boots. I opened the top three snaps down the front and headed over to Toni's place.

* * * * *

Toni's town house, a modern red brick building, faced College Street, a busy four-lane road that bordered the western side of the FCU campus. I parked on a side street a few blocks away for fear that Julia might spot my car.

I arrived at three o'clock, right on time.

"Hey, cowgirl, you're looking hot today," Toni said to me as I walked in the door. Wearing cutoff jeans so short that the pockets hung out the bottom and a Texas Rangers baseball shirt, Toni gave me a provocative look that registered in my crotch.

"I was nervous about backing onto College," I said, "so I parked a few blocks away." Lying was starting to become second nature to me.

Toni smiled. "Let me just stick the quiche in the oven. Make yourself at home."

The first floor of the town house was tidy and spacious, thanks to a high ceiling and skylight. White rugs were scattered over the hardwood floor. I sat down on a white leather sofa next to the red brick fireplace and looked around. A large metal bookcase held Toni's law books, stereo, and television. In the dining area, above the table, a print of Picasso's *Les Demoiselles d'Avignon* dominated the wall. A spiral staircase led upstairs.

Toni returned from the kitchen with a bottle of white wine.

"This place is great," I said. "How do you keep it so nice?"

"I have somebody come in and clean once a week. Mom and Dad think of the place as an investment.

They hope to sell it for a big profit when I finish law school," she said. "Care for some Sonoma chardonnay? I also have some French champagne and a nice little Napa sauvignon blanc."

"The chardonnay sounds nice," I said. "But just one glass. I'm driving."

"Oh no. You're going to be here a while, my dear," she said, giving me a seductive look that again produced ripples of lust in me.

"Where do you study?" I said.

"Upstairs, in the spare bedroom. Do you want to see?"

"Okay," I said, following her up the spiral staircase, trying my best not to stare at her ass.

She led me to her office, where she had a drafting table, desk and IBM computer.

"This must be convenient," I said.

She left the office and led me to her sprawling bedroom, with platform bed and modern Danish dresser, bureau and nightstand.

"Well, what do you think?" she said, standing very near me, so close I could smell her.

"Looks comfortable," I said.

"Want to try it out?" Her meaning was unmistakable.

My heart in my throat, my lust nearly out of control, I was just about to grab Toni and kiss her hard and desperately, for all those years I had wanted her.

Just then, there was a knock at the door.

"Oh, that's probably my brother," she said. "Wait up here. He just wanted to borrow something. I'll get rid of him in two minutes."

Toni ran downstairs to answer the door, and I sat on the edge of the bed. From there, I could hear her conversation with Paul.

"Here's the money," she said. "That should tide you over until Mom sends the checks."

"Thanks, Toni. You're a real pal," he said. "Listen, do you have a minute. I really need to talk to you. I'm in deep shit."

"Paul, I have a guest right now. Can it wait till later?"

"I guess," he said peevishly. "Who is it?"

"An old friend. She's upstairs."

"A girl? Just get rid of her, for God's sake. I need to talk." His tone was whiny.

"Paul, I'll call you tonight, okay?"

I heard Toni shut the door and then run back up the stairs. By the time she reached the doorway, she had unbuttoned her top. "Sorry about that interruption," she said, dropping her shirt to the floor. "He can be very demanding sometimes, but he's my kid brother. What can I do?" She reached out and started unsnapping my shirt.

"I've got to go." I looked away and stood up.

"Oh come on, Carmen. I thought this was what you wanted."

"I do. But I can't," I said, my heart in my throat.

"Julia will never know unless you tell her."

"I'm sorry," I said. I left Toni standing in the bedroom.

* * * * *

42

When I came home, Charles, decked out in a bright yellow Hawaiian-print shirt and khaki slacks, was making a snack in the kitchen. "You're just in time. I'm having a quick sandwich before I head out to the bars. I decided to go tropical. You want a sandwich?"

"Where's Julia?" I said, still throbbing with lust and panting and sweating from nervousness and guilt.

"She has a seminar tonight. Don't you keep up with your own wife's schedule?"

I said nothing.

"Do you have a straw hat I can borrow?"

I shook my head.

"Hey, what's with the black outfit? Have you been to a Johnny Cash Fan Club meeting?"

"Charles, I've got to talk to you, and I have to swear you to absolute secrecy." I sat at the kitchen table and buried my head in my hands.

"Of course I won't tell," he said. "Did you rob a bank?"

I looked up at him. "Oh God, you won't believe the day I've had." I held my index finger and thumb about an inch apart. "I just came this close to having sex with Toni. Her brother dropped by just as I was getting ready to jump her. That startled me enough for my sanity to return — temporarily at least."

Charles put down his sandwich and regarded me grimly.

"She's selfish, cruel, shallow and manipulative," I said. "But when I'm in the same room with her, I'm so drawn to her. There's something about her. The way she carries herself. The way she moves. She's like a fantasy. What's wrong with me?"

Charles didn't answer.

"You know, if she'd just said she loved me back then, I might have spent the rest of my life with her."

"If she had said she loved you," he said, "she would have been a different person."

"What am I going to do?" I said.

"That's up to you." He sat down next to me. "I've known you eight years. You were miserable the whole time you were with Toni, and you were even worse off with Jane. Finally, you've found a fantastic woman who loves you dearly. And for the past two years you've been really happy, Carmen. If you want to risk that just because you have a throb in your crotch for some piece of gutter trash, that's your business."

I said nothing.

"Do you still love Julia? Or have you completely lost your mind?"

"Yes, of course, I love her," I said.

"Then pull yourself together and stay away from that tramp." He patted me on the back. "By the way, nice perfume. Opium?"

It was nine-thirty when Julia, looking tall and beautiful in her Levis, white Oxford shirt and tennis shoes, returned from her seminar. I met her at the front door.

"We need to talk," I said, leading her to the bedroom.

She put down her knapsack and sat on the bed with me. "This sounds serious. You're scaring me, Carmen." She gave me a cautious look.

"I'm sorry, baby," I said, softly stroking her hand. "I've been neglecting you, and I'm not going to do it anymore. You're the most important person in my life. I want you to know that I love you and I want to be with you. Just you."

"You saw Toni today." She looked directly at me, her green eyes hard and angry.

Averting my gaze, I nodded my head.

She pulled her hand away. "Dear God, I knew it. It's been written all over you ever since you saw her that night."

"Julia, baby, I swear to God nothing happened between us today."

"I don't want to know about it." She held her hand up. "You made me feel like I was making an idiot of myself."

"I'm sorry," I said, helplessly.

"Just give me some time alone." Julia began crying with long heaving sobs, her shoulders shaking with grief and rage.

"I allowed myself to be distracted, temporarily, but I won't do it anymore. I promise." I put my arm around her to comfort her.

"Don't touch me, Carmen. You lied to me today, and that's something I never thought you'd do. I don't want to see you right now," she said, her voice soft yet trembling with fury. I had never seen her like this before, but I knew she would not be swayed.

For the next several hours, I drove around — all the while punishing myself over my dalliance with Toni and my lies to Julia.

I slapped the steering wheel as I thought of Julia — hurt and disappointed. "Dear God, what was I thinking of?" I said as I headed north along Highway Seventy-five.

Whatever strong attraction I felt for Toni, it wasn't worth the pain I had caused Julia, my lover and dearest friend. When I passed the Kansas border, I turned around and headed back to Frontier City.

I got home at three a.m. All the lights were out, and Charles was fast asleep on the sofa bed with both cats curled up around him. I tiptoed through the living room, careful not to wake them.

Once in the bedroom, I sat on the bed and slipped off my shoes.

"I'm still awake, Carmen." Julia said, her voice showing no emotion.

"Are you all right?" I said softly.

"I've been better. Where were you? I was worried."

"I drove around," I said. "I ended in Kansas, up around Caney, of all places." I stretched out beside her on the bed. "It's not much of a drive at night, or during the day either, for that matter."

"I'm glad you came back," she said. "I missed you."

My heart ached. "I'm very sorry, Julia, sorry for lying to you, sorry for making you doubt me. You have every right to be angry at me. I was selfish and short-sighted. But, I promise, if you give me another chance, I won't let you down. Please, I want you to trust me again. I love you, and I don't want to lose you."

"I love you too," Julia said. "And I want to trust you. I really want to. Let's give it some time."

I held her until we both fell asleep.

CHAPTER THREE

The October air was cool as I pulled into the driveway. It was Julia's turn to run the meeting, so the coalition was meeting at our apartment. Guilt and shame flooded me as I spotted Toni's red BMW out front. We hadn't spoken since my visit to her town house two weeks ago. She hadn't called me, and I hadn't called her.

Julia hadn't talked about Toni since the night I drove to Kansas, except to mention, icily, that she hadn't shown up at the weekly meetings.

My relationship with Julia had never been so

distant. There were long, uncomfortable silences between us and our sex life was non-existent.

I steeled myself to face Toni.

"I'm going to have to institute a no-smoking rule in this house," I heard Julia say to the group as I walked in.

"Good evening, all," I said as I walked in. My heart lurched when I saw Toni, forever cool, tonight wearing her battered black leather biker jacket. I remembered the first day I saw her in that jacket. We'd met for lunch in the Student Union cafeteria, and when I spotted her across the room, I nearly passed out from a combination of repressed lust and terror.

I longed for the day that I could see this woman with indifference.

Toni looked up at me — a fleeting look of pleasure passing over her face. Perhaps she sensed the turmoil she provoked in me.

"Smoking's not a big issue with me," Toni said. "I can go without a cig for a couple of hours."

Leonard — wearing another all-black outfit, this one topped by a military-style beret — ignored me. He probably ordered his outfits from the Che Guevara Young Revolutionaries' catalog. "Hey, it's an issue for me," he said, shooting the group a petulant look. "I can't think without a cigarette."

Donna — a tall, lean woman with short curly black hair and intense, dark eyes — cleared her throat. "Excuse me, but I haven't gotten to talk all night. And I'm sorry for making the meeting run over even more, Julia, but since nine-thirty when I got here, we've done nothing but listen to Leonard —"

"The meeting started at nine." Leonard folded his thin arms over his chest. "If you had shown up on time —"

"You know I have rehearsals," Donna said. "And that brings up another point. I agree with Julia about the cigarettes."

Tom nodded, entering the fray. A slight, swarthy man with black hair and black eyes, he was a second-generation Mexican-American from Dallas. "I also agree about the cigarettes. And about these long meetings. We need to finish on time. My workload it really tough this semester. I don't have time to sit here three-plus hours every Tuesday night. Let's plan some events, get funding and recognition from the student government —"

"You people don't care about anything important, do you?" Leonard shouted. "This is a life-and-death struggle. In the words of Malcolm X, 'By any means necessary.' "

"Can you cut the slogans for just a second and start listening for a change?" Tom said, his voice rising, his eyes turning fierce. He pushed up the sleeves of his gray Dallas Cowboys sweat shirt and leaned toward Leonard. "First and foremost, I'm here for an education. And that doesn't make me a sellout. I'm the first in my family to go to college. I need good grades to keep my scholarship."

Leonard sat silently, his face peevish.

"Homophobia isn't an abstract concept to me," Tom continued. "I've been called faggot and *maricón* on the street. I've had my butt kicked because of the way I look, the way I carry myself. You've got to drop this macho, controlling bullshit."

Toni slammed her hand on the table. "Why

doesn't everybody just fucking chill out? Jesus. Leonard, just stop smoking at the meetings, okay? Don't make a fucking Greek drama out of it."

The room was silent. Nauseous from watching the conflict, I used the pause to retreat to the bedroom.

Charles was sprawled on my bed, Walkman headphones clamped to his head, book in hand, and cats plastered to his lap.

My stomach churning from the turmoil in the living room, I sat next to him on the bed.

"What a group," I said.

"I'm afraid I set Leonard off," Charles said guiltily. "I've been dodging his calls for weeks. I thought it was kinder just to avoid him. I thought he would get the message. Tonight when I came in, he cornered me and demanded that I go outside with him."

"Oh jeez."

"He just wouldn't let me break it to him gently. I told him I was really busy with my dissertation, that I didn't have time to date, that I was going back to California, that I didn't want to get involved with anybody. I really tried to be nice."

"So what happened?" I said, my nausea worsening.

"He basically threw himself at me. He said he would make it easy for me, that he wouldn't make a lot of demands. He even promised to cook for me. He even said — God this is really embarrassing —"

"You don't have to tell me," I said, hoping he wouldn't.

He ignored me. When Charles was in his storytelling mode, he was unstoppable. He lowered his voice to a whisper. "He said he would just give me a back rub if that's all I wanted to do." Charles groaned. "Finally, I had to tell him flat out that I didn't want to see *him*. And then he started crying. I spent the better part of an hour calming him down, trying to build his confidence back up. I told him he shouldn't sell himself short, that there are a lot of guys out there who would be interested in him."

"I've heard that speech plenty of times before," I said.

Charles continued: "I convinced him to go back into the meeting. He's been a pill since then, taking his anger out on them instead of me. That guy is full of rage. Even the cats are freaked out." He patted Holly, who purred appreciatively.

"I know what he feels like. I've been there," I said. "How's Julia doing with Toni here?"

"She's a class act. She treated Toni with perfect civility," Charles said.

A few minutes later, Leonard shouted shrilly, his voice ragged, "None of you knows what I'm about. None of you!"

Charles and I ran into the living room. By then, Donna and Tom had left.

"You're outta line, pal," Toni said to Leonard.

"You have an awful lot to say for somebody who's only come to two meetings," Leonard shot back at her.

"Like your opinion of me matters," Toni retorted.

"Hey, hold on here," Julia said. "Let's not make the situation any worse than what it is, Toni. Leonard, we need your support and cooperation."

"Stop kissing his ass, Julia. You're only giving him more power," Toni said. Then she squared off to face Leonard. "Leonard, you're being ridiculous.

Whether you come back or not, this group will survive just fine. And if you do come back, why don't you listen to what everyone else in the group is telling you to do?"

"Oh, and what would that be?" Leonard said snidely.

"Drop the filibustering. Or let me put it in terms even you can understand. Shut up for a change."

"You fucking bitch," Leonard spat back.

Toni sneered. "That really hurts, coming from a someone like you."

"Please, Toni. That's enough," I said. Leonard was way out of his depth. He had provoked a shrewd woman with a mean streak a mile wide. Unchecked, she would go for the kill.

"Relax, Carmen," Toni said. "I'm just saying what everybody else here wants to. Only I'm not as polite as the rest of you."

"Oh really? I thought you rich cunts were supposed to have beautiful manners," Leonard said.

Charles and I looked at each other, too stunned to speak.

"Goddamnit, just stop it, both of you," Julia said. "You're destroying something we're working hard to build. If you want to fight like this, do it somewhere else."

Unfazed, Toni leaned in toward Leonard, her cruel, cold face only inches away from his. "Everybody knows you're just putting on a big, macho display because you want to get Charlie in the sack. Well, he's way out of your league, psycho."

Charles blushed and then let out an embarrassed laugh.

Leonard was taken aback. Then, tears welled in

his eyes. "How could you do this to me, Charles?" he said. Then he stormed out, slamming the door behind him.

"We'd better go after him," Charles said. "Come on, Julia. I don't want to be alone with him again."

After they left, Toni and I stood alone in the living room.

Offering a sly smile, Toni said, "Hey, long time no see, babe. Where've you been?"

I looked at her, her face calm and composed. She seemed oblivious to the melodrama around her. "I've been here, at home, where I belong," I said, more than a little self-righteously. "I'm surprised you came here tonight. What did you want to do — taunt Julia? And when she wouldn't take the bait, you went after Leonard. Right?"

"Oh please. What happened between us had nothing to do with Julia. You came to my house. Remember?" She put her hands on her hips and cocked her head slightly. "Let's face it. We wasted the three years we had together. You and I both know that we should have been lovers. But we were too scared or stupid or repressed to do anything about it back then. So four years passed, and we grew up. I wanted one chance to be with you sexually. You wanted it too."

I ignored the comment, unable to look at her.

"You don't have to hate me for making a pass at you. I didn't want to break you and Julia up. Julia seems like a really nice woman. I'm glad you have her in your life. I like you, Carmen. . . . No. That's a weak way of saying it. I'll never feel about anybody else the way I feel about you."

I couldn't respond.

Suddenly, tears filled her eyes and her voice grew passionate. "I thought I'd never see you again. I never forgot you, Carmen. I made a lot of mistakes a long time ago. Okay? I know I hurt you. But we're together again. That's a miracle. Sex between us now would be mistake. But it would be a shame to let our friendship slip away again." She wiped her eyes on the sleeve of her leather jacket.

She was right. I shouldn't hate her for what happened during senior year or for the pass she'd made at me; we'd both been a party to all of it. At last, I could see the real Toni — beyond the cowboy boots, the leather jacket, the cigarettes, the cool slang and the posturing. She was vulnerable. But angry at myself for still being attracted to her, I was in no mood to be conciliatory. "Why did you fight with Leonard like that?" I said. "It's beneath you, Toni."

"Oh come on. This isn't Sunday school, Carmen. He called me filthy names, and I put him in his place. Be glad I didn't deck him," she said. She was trying to sound cocky, but her hands were trembling.

I glared at her. "You didn't have to make the comment about his crush on Charles. You destroyed him, Toni. It's like dropping a nuclear bomb on a schoolyard bully."

"I don't get you, Carmen. I was standing up to a jerk who treated your girlfriend and her friends like shit, and all you can do is tell me that I'm in the wrong," she said, her tears returning.

Something in me hardened. I wanted to hurt her for all the years of frustration and anguish she had caused me. "You don't give a damn about what you did to Julia's group. You only care about yourself."

"Thanks for the psychoanalysis, Doc," she said. "I'll mail you a check for the session." And with that, she took off into the night.

Suddenly, I felt hot tears running down my cheeks. Toni was right. We were still lost at the carnival. And we just missed finding each other. Again.

Julia and Charles returned about an hour later. They had tracked Leonard down at his apartment, but he had refused to see them.

The next Tuesday, after work, I found Charles on the sofa, but no Julia.

"She's not back from the meeting yet?" I said.

"She and Tom swept by about an hour ago," he said, looking up from his book. As usual, the cats had stationed themselves at either side of him. "They're looking for Leonard. They stopped by to see whether he had come by here. Julia hung out long enough to give me all the dirt."

"Looking for him?" I said, sitting down in the rocking chair across from him.

Putting down his book, Charles leaned toward me. "Well, you know, the meeting was supposed to be at his apartment, which was dark when they got there. They knocked for about five minutes and there was no answer. So they left a note on his door and met in the Student Union. They thought maybe he forgot or was just running late, but he never showed. After the meeting, they checked his place again, and he was still gone. Donna went back to her dorm, in case he tried to call."

"I don't get it."

"Well, you see, Leonard and Toni got in a huge blowout at Wilde's last night."

Wilde's was a year-old gay bar in the university district. The clientele was mostly gay men, although on any given night, about a quarter of the patrons were lesbians. The rest was a sprinkling of curious straights. Julia and I had been there once. The place was loud, flashy and frenetic; most of the patrons were there to cruise. Wilde's was closer to home, but we were loyal to Crystal's Tavern, the only women's bar in town. I had become friends with the owner, Crystal Reeves, a couple of years back through my work at the newspaper.

"So what happened?" I said, growing impatient. Charles liked to milk a story, but I was in no mood for one of his Broadway productions.

"Oh, this is too much, Carmen," he said, waving his hands as he spoke. "Donna told Julia that she and Leonard went to the bar together. Leonard spotted Toni, so he tried to talk to her. She just brushed him off totally. He started to raise hell, so Toni went to the bartender and had Leonard bounced from the bar. He was very angry, shouting, 'I'll get you, you fucking bitch.' They literally dragged him out of the place."

"Great," I said.

"Nobody's seen Leonard, and of course Toni didn't show up at the meeting tonight. Apparently, she only shows up at the meetings at your place. I guess there's a certain ex-admirer she wants to keep stirred up."

So Toni had made a special effort to see *me*. I was embarrassed, yet somehow pleased.

"That's not the worst of it. Leonard called me again today. The man has absolutely no pride," Charles said, rubbing his forehead in exasperation. "He asked me if we could just be friends. He was begging, for God's sake."

"What did you do?"

"I told him no. I'm sad for him, but the worst thing I could do for him right now is hang out with him. I suggested he get some counseling. That seemed to infuriate him."

"Damn," I said.

"You know, he's really angry. Every time I reject him, he gets worse."

I shook my head. Leonard was a mental health disaster.

The next night, I was on the much-despised overnight shift. I arrived at eight p.m. Wednesday and was required to stay until four in the morning. My duties were to check the wires for breaking news, monitor the police scanner, make sure no major mistakes were printed in the final edition of the paper, stop the presses in case of earth-shattering events and organize coverage on the off chance City Hall got bombed by the Russians. In reality, I just sat there all night with little to do, because nothing ever happened.

The newsroom — vast and modern with dove-gray desks, sea-green carpet and blue walls — pulsed with activity for most of the day. In the morning and afternoon, reporters emerged from their cubicles to haggle with their assignment editors, who worked from one of two central desks — state or metro. In the evening, the layout and copy editors came in — working from two huge horseshoe-shaped desks. From there, we molded the individual stories and photographs assembled that day into the final product readers saw the next morning. We printed 150,000 copies Monday through Saturday. On Sundays, circulation swelled to 225,000. The *Times* dominated Frontier City, eastern Oklahoma and western Arkansas. Our only major opposition was *The Herald,* an afternoon paper less than half our size that was perennially on the verge of collapse. The Oklahoma City papers, content to dominate the western half of the state, ceded the east to us.

I had Jerry Newman, my new boss, to thank for this odious shift. Newman, a humorless martinet in his late thirties who had been hired away from an Oklahoma City newspaper, had replaced Ralph Sargent, who had retired four months ago.

Sargent, big, brash and tyrannical, had run the copy desk with Marine Corps discipline and subjected new editors to public ridicule as part of his boot camp. After four months of Newman, the very people Sargent had abused and tormented now missed him desperately. Now we remembered him fondly and selectively. We recalled his sense of humor and late-night drinking sessions at Bailey's Bar and overlooked his brutal tirades and vicious sarcasm.

Exhibiting no signs or a personality, social skills

or a life outside of the office, Newman was uncomfortable with me from the outset. Soon after he was hired, he had a one-on-one conference with each member of the copy desk.

When my turn came up, Newman — a tall, thin man with thinning brown hair — was a wreck. "I'm very familiar with your reputation, Carmen," he said, fiddling with his wire-rim glasses as sweat beaded on his forehead.

"Oh yeah?" I said lightly. "And is that good or bad?"

"That depends on what kind of attitude you take out of this meeting. I've been through your personnel file and talked to your superiors, and I hope we can avoid the kinds of incidents that have happened in the past."

I suspected what he was hinting at. A couple of years back, I had taken a visible stand against a homophobic series the paper was set to run. Ultimately, I was vindicated, but my position had brought me into direct conflict with Sargent and other high-ranking editors. More importantly, it had outed me in a less-than-queer-friendly newsroom.

Many of my co-workers avoided me; others, hoping to convert me, invited me to church; still others preferred to ignore my sexual orientation. And, of course, there was John Gruber's approach.

Gruber, a pudgy copy editor who quivered every time he came near me, had asked me out on dates five times a week for about a year. After my work on the series, he subjected me to the National Standardized Quiz for Lesbians.

Gruber: How do you know you're *that way?*

Me: Trust me. I just do.

Gruber: How do you know you haven't met the right man?

Me: How do you know you're straight? Maybe you just haven't met the right man.

Gruber (with husky voice and bedroom eyes): I can be very sensitive. You know? Give it a try. Just once. What could it hurt? I know what you girls do. I've seen it in magazines and videos.

Me (with my fiercest Bette Davis withering glare): I'm not interested in you at all and I never will be. Period. I don't care how many whack-off magazines you've read. Got it?

After that exchange, our relationship made the Cold War look like a church social, but over the last few months, Gruber started dating a nurse he had met at an all-night diner. Bolstered by his new-found love, he had begun making friendly overtures toward me. I wasn't one to bear a grudge forever. Besides, I certainly knew what it was like to be obsessed with a woman I couldn't have.

But Jerry Newman was far tougher to handle.

"I have a good reputation here, Jerry. I've been here coming up on three years. The Barrett case put me on the map. I was commended for my work," I reminded him in a calm voice. "I even got a bonus. If you don't believe me, ask Ralph Sargent."

"Sargent can't shield you anymore. This is my ship now, and I'm going to run it a lot tighter than he did."

That would be hard to imagine.

His eyes shifted. "Everyone here starts with a clean slate, but clean slates must be kept clean. I want good, solid copy editors who don't have an agenda."

"What kind of agenda?" I said.

He avoided my eyes. "You know what I'm referring to."

I stood up. "If you have something to say to me, say it flat out." Did Newman have the guts to say that he wouldn't tolerate an out dyke on the copy desk? Is that even what he was hinting at or was I just being paranoid?

Silent, Newman pulled a handkerchief from his pocket and wiped his glasses.

"My only agenda is to come in here and do a professional job. I stand up for what I think is right. Copy editors are hired to think, Jerry, not just to be grammarians. I hope that isn't a problem."

"We'll see about that," he said.

From then on, I had been on his shit list, editing obits, briefs, farm page copy. And predictably, I wound up on the overnight shift far more often than any other copy editor.

At one a.m., I was alone in the newsroom. Gary, the overnight clerk who shared this hateful shift with me, was downstairs in the mail room picking up copies of the final edition of the paper. Despite the fact that he was a Lovell Taft University freshman who brought his Bible to read during his spare moments, we got along well. We had an unspoken agreement. He didn't try to convert me and I didn't pick holes in his literal reading of the Bible. Besides, for a fundamentalist Christian, he had an offbeat, irreverent sense of humor. I was scanning the state news wire when the phone rang.

"I've got to talk to you." It was Toni. Loud music pulsed in the background.

"How did you know to reach me here?" I said.

"Julia told me. I tried you at home first."

Julia? God, what would she think? I pushed the thought out of my head. "What's going on with you and Leonard?" I asked.

"Oh, that little worm. You know he flattened my tires? At least I think it was him. I found them that way this morning. And today, he called me up to tell me he was going to get even with me. Like I'd be scared of him."

I looked up. Gary placed two copies of the final edition on my desk. I nodded and mouthed "thanks" at him; he replied with a deep curtsy and then a whimsical little wave. More than once, I had wondered whether Gary was gay.

"This feud is getting you nowhere. You guys should bury the hatchet — if only for the sake of the group."

"That's vintage Carmen — always the little Sunday school teacher at heart. Well, you can forget it. Leonard and I aren't going to kiss and make up."

She was right. They'd both gone too far. The best thing to hope for was complete separation, but which one would leave the group? I wasn't going to butt into that dispute. That was up to Julia and the rest of her group. "Listen, I'd really like to talk, but I've got to check the final edition."

"Hold on a sec. This is business. I have a news tip for you. Carmen, you're the only person I know in the media. I'm onto a very big story, but if I give it to you, you have to promise to protect somebody involved."

"You have my word," I said. I cleared my

computer screen and started a new file, which I named "TONI," in my personal queue so that I could take notes. "Go on."

"Oops. Sorry. Gotta. They're leaving. I'll call you tomorrow with the details." And with that, the phone went dead.

After I quickly transcribed our conversation, I looked out across the empty newsroom as I thought about Toni. She was still reaching out to me, even after the way I had acted the last time we saw each other. Maybe we *could* finally be friends — if we exercised maturity and restraint.

When Toni called back with her news tip, I would apologize for my rudeness.

And Julia? Eventually, she could come to accept a Platonic friendship between me and Toni. Sure, I was still attracted to her, but I didn't have to act on those feelings. I would give Julia plenty of time to get used to the idea. As long as I was completely honest with her, what could go wrong?

The next day, I woke up when I heard the front door open. I glanced at the clock. It was two p.m., Thursday, time for Julia to be back from school.

I shuffled into the kitchen, where I found her making coffee. I sat down at the table and looked at her. To me, she was always, quite simply, beautiful. She was wearing a green sweater, which brought out the color of her eyes, and gray wool slacks.

"I don't want you to think anything fishy is going on with Toni," I said. "She called because she had a news tip for me. I don't want you to think I was doing something behind your back."

"Carmen, you told me I could trust you. For me, it's a closed issue," Julia said, her face calm and open.

I knew she was being honest. I smiled at her.

"Would you like me to make you some breakfast or lunch or whatever you eat after working such a horrendous shift?" she offered.

I shook my head. "No thanks. What I would really like is for you to come over here."

"*Moi?*" she said, walking toward me.

"Yes," I said, pulling her onto my lap. "I don't have to be at work until eight o'clock. Charles left this morning and won't be back until late tonight."

"And?" Julia said.

"Don't you think it's time we stopped being strangers? Way back when, we used to be lovers. Remember?"

"Yes, I remember," Julia said. "I think it's time."

"Then, please, let me do everything," I said. "I want all of this to be for you."

Closing her eyes, Julia nodded at me.

I began kissing her neck, slowly, the way she liked it.

Slipping my hand under her sweater, I stroked the warm, soft skin along her spine as I continued to kiss her neck lightly.

Julia moaned quietly and then met my lips with a tender kiss that ignited passion inside me.

I could easily have devoted my entire life just to kissing her.

Determined that Julia should have everything she

wanted, I took my time, gently stroking her back, her face and her hair, all the while kissing her neck and mouth as she sat on my lap. I unzipped her pants, and slid my hand down her back, near but not yet touching her butt.

With one hand I touched her breasts, first one, then the other. Meanwhile, with the other hand, I moved down to fondle her cheeks.

Because her breasts were always very sensitive, I caressed only the sides. At last, she cried out in frustration, so I began working on her nipples with my mouth. At first, I offered only gentle kisses, but Julia grew more demanding, so I sucked and licked them, harder and harder, until her breasts were rosy from all the attention lavished on them.

I moved my hand down her belly to the top of her pubic hair as I continued to suck and lick her exquisite breasts. Flirting and teasing, I lightly massaged her pubic hair until, at last, I dipped one finger into her wetness. Julia gasped. Making slow, gentle circles around her clitoris with my middle finger, grasping her cheeks with my other hand, I continued working on Julia's breasts, sucking, licking, and now nibbling them.

Her breathing grew more urgent, her movements more demanding, her wetness incredible. I knew what she wanted, what she needed.

I told her to stand up, take off her pants and go sit on the edge of the couch.

First moving the coffee table out of the way, I dropped to the floor in front of her and buried my face between her legs, eagerly lapping up her generous supply of cream. As I sensed her growing closer to climax, I pulled back, wanting to give her more pleasure, wanting her to wait.

I stopped licking her and stuck one finger inside her. Moaning, Julia drove herself down onto my hand. I added a second finger and then a third, slowly moving in and out of her. When I resumed licking and sucking her, Julia's breathing grew frantic.

Within moments, she came.

She was so aroused that I kept my mouth between her legs, kissing her gently at first, then licking and sucking her again. A few minutes later, she came again.

Then I led her into the bedroom and told her to lie on her stomach.

Slowly and carefully as I crouched over her, I kissed her neck, back and shoulders as Julia, now relaxed, lay still.

After smothering my hands with lotion, I massaged her back, working my way down. Finally, I reached her cheeks, which I rubbed and stroked lovingly and firmly. Julia began to moan. She was aroused again.

I asked her to turn over, and then I kissed her deeply on the mouth.

"I love you so much," I said, my heart nearly bursting with the intense passion I felt for her.

"Is it my turn yet?" Julia asked.

"All in good time, my pretty. All in good time," I said. "I have a lot more in store for you."

* * * * *

After making love to Julia for hours, I drove to work. It was a clear, moonless night in the city, and traffic on the Crosstown Highway, a spur of Interstate 44, was light. My heart was overwhelmed by the devotion and tenderness I felt for Julia.

My commitment to her was clear and strong. I would never let anyone else interfere with that. I knew that for certain.

CHAPTER FOUR

By Saturday, I still hadn't heard from Toni. And neither had anyone else. She hadn't shown up for classes and no one had seen her around campus. Her car was gone. The campus security force contacted her parents, who lived in The Village, a wealthy suburb of Oklahoma City. They hadn't heard from her in the last two weeks. And Bradley hadn't seen her in three weeks.

I wasn't overly worried. A handful of times during our friendship, Toni had taken off without a word to anyone and stayed gone until she wanted to come back. I expected her to turn up any day with a wild story about why she had disappeared.

It was early Thursday morning. Toni had called me a week ago and hadn't been heard from since. I was more than halfway through the overnight shift. To pass the time, I was editing a long wire story about heart attacks for the Sunday paper when the police scanner distracted me.

". . . Body of a twenty-six-year-old Caucasian female. All units in the Cherokee Park area, please respond," the dispatcher said.

My heart froze. Toni? I looked up at the clock. It was two a.m.

My legs trembling, I ran to the library, where I found Gary, the overnight clerk, reading his Bible.

"What's up, boss? Everything okay?" he said.

"I want you to call the police. See if you can track down the ID of a twenty-six-year-old woman found dead at Cherokee Park," I said, trying to keep the panic out of my voice.

Frontier City had more than its share of trouble spots — Cherokee Park among its worst. Surely Toni, as street-smart as she was, would have the sense to steer clear of that dangerous area, I told myself.

"Can it wait till I finish this chapter?"

"No," I said, terror rising in me.

"It's too late to get anything into the final edition."

"Gary, I gave you an assignment, God damn it. I'm ranking editor in the building. Move your ass. Now." I realized that I was shrieking, but I didn't care. I couldn't. Not until I knew that Toni was all right.

Blushing a deep red, Gary ran from the library to the newsroom and got on the phone.

It was three-thirty when Gary got back to me. Sitting in the receptionist's darkened office in the newsroom foyer, I hoped my gut reaction had been wrong. Over and over, I told myself that the victim could be anyone from anywhere. Not Toni. Please, God, not Toni.

"What are you doing out here, chief?" Gary said, approaching sheepishly.

"Do you have the ID?" I said, my heart in my throat.

"Yeah. They were really giving me the runaround. They wouldn't tell me until the family had been notified."

"Get on with it," I said.

"Our lucky stiff is Antoinette —"

"Victoria Stewart," I said.

"Did you know her?" Gary asked.

"Oh dear God, no. It's Toni."

"I'm so sorry. Is there anything I can do? Someone I can call?" he said.

"Please, just leave me alone," I said.

I wept uncontrollably for the better part of an hour.

I have no recollection of how I got home.

* * * * *

Acting on an anonymous tip, police found Toni's body in a wooded area by Lake Sequoyah, a manmade lake in Frontier City's sprawling north side Cherokee Park. She had been dead about a week, a victim of homicide.

Four days after her body was found, Toni's funeral was held on a cold, rainy Monday in a suburb of Oklahoma City. Julia, Charles and I made the ninety-mile trip along Interstate Forty-Four in silence. My Civic couldn't seat six, so Donna, Tom and Leonard followed in Leonard's black sixty-seven Volkswagen Bug.

The service, held in a funeral home chapel and presided over by a young Presbyterian minister, was a blur. Words about resurrection and eternal life and God's mercy flowed past my ears without registering. All I could focus on was the pain clawing at my chest and the tears pouring down my face.

At the cemetery, under slate gray skies, the minister uttered the benediction, commending Toni's soul to God. I joined the line of mourners streaming past the grave. Each placed a white rose on the casket before she was lowered into the earth.

"Goodbye, Toni," I said as I dropped the flower onto her casket. "Thanks for everything."

After the rites concluded, I approached her parents. To me, they had always seemed an elegant couple. I had met them a couple of times on their visits to Frontier City. Toni's comments about her parents always concentrated on facts, not on feelings. Like much of the rest of Toni's life, Mr. and Mrs. Stewart were a mystery to me. Toni strongly resembled Mrs. Stewart, except that her mother was older, softer and more elegant-looking. Mr. Stewart was a tall, distinguished silver-haired man in his late fifties. They were preparing to get into the limousine when I approached.

"Mr. and Mrs. Stewart," I said, "I'm so sorry about Toni."

"Oh, Carmen, thank you for coming," said Mrs. Stewart, reaching out and hugging me. Her husband, impassive, stood at her side. "It's been so long since we've seen you, dear."

I offered Mr. Stewart my hand, but he must have been too distracted to notice. Finally, I pulled it back. "I just wanted to tell you that Toni was a very good friend to me, back when we were in college," I said. "We had so much fun together, and I'm so glad that I got a chance to enjoy those times with her. She'll always mean a lot to me."

"Oh, thank you, dear," Mrs. Stewart said.

"Where's Paul? I'd like to say something to him."

The father seemed lost in his own thoughts. "He's back at the house," Mrs. Stewart said. "He was so shaken that he had to be sedated. They were very, very close."

Yes, she had loved him a great deal, I thought. Tears filled my eyes again. "Please give him my deepest sympathy."

"Of course, dear," she said. "Have you spoken to Bradley? I think he's taken it hardest of all. He and Toni were to be married this summer."

For a moment, I was stunned. "I didn't get to speak with him yet. Again, I am sorry."

She embraced me again, and then I left.

* * * * *

I waited by the car as the rest of our party offered their condolences. A few young mourners — friends from Toni's childhood or perhaps from FCU — dotted the assembly. I didn't know any of them. Many of them made their way toward the Stewarts. And then finally, I noticed Bradley, wearing a black suit and dark glasses. Standing over her grave, he shook with grief. I would speak with him, but I couldn't manage it yet.

Just then, Leonard approached me. His pale face was puffy and torn with grief. "How can I ever forgive myself, Carmen?" he said weakly. He began to weep bitterly. "Oh, dear God, I'm so sorry," he said, over and over.

Back on the highway, I broke the grim silence in the car. "Toni was planning to marry Bradley this summer. At least that's what she was telling her parents."

Charles, stone-faced, stared at the farmland racing past us. Julia fiddled with the highway map.

"I guess there's a lot about Toni we don't know," I said, gripping the steering wheel as tears filled my eyes again.

Julia put her arm around me. I bit my lower lip and drove on.

That day, after I drove home from the funeral, I dropped by to see Terry Harris, whom I had known since our days as journalism students at FCU. After three years as a police reporter, she had been promoted to senior crime reporter last year — thanks to her huge network of sources. She occasionally dated cops and knew where most of the department's bodies were buried. Not given to humility, Terry bragged that she knew what the police chief was going to have for lunch before he even opened his menu. An attractive woman with permed, shoulder-length brunette hair, she pounded her keyboard as she composed a story. "Jesus! Fuck!"

"Hi, Terry. How goes it?"

"What is it now, Miss Copy Desk? Did I miss a semicolon in one of my stories?" She paused to shove a wedge of pimento-cheese-spread sandwich in her mouth.

"This is serious."

"I'm on deadline," she said, still chewing. "I've got to file this story in fifteen minutes."

"A friend of mine was murdered." I filled her in on the few details I knew about the case, including that final phone call. "Can you find out what the cops know on this case?"

"I'll get right on it. And listen, this one is on the house."

Tuesday, Terry called as I was getting ready for work.

"Carmen," she said, "how close were you to this woman? This isn't pretty."

"It's all right. Give it to me," I said. I steeled myself. I owed it to Toni to know how she died.

"I called a friend over at the coroner's office," Terry began matter-of-factly. "The victim was beaten to death. It was a massive case of overkill — multiple blows, all over the body. The skull was crushed. The coroner had to use dental records for a positive ID."

The words rolled past me. I understood them, but I would not allow them to register emotionally.

She continued, "The police combed the north end of the lake. That part of the park is pretty remote — you can only reach it by boat or by a rugged three-mile wooded trail. The cops think she was killed in a small clearing about fifty yards away, then dumped in the woods." She paused. "Oh, no murder weapon yet, but they're still looking. What else? No signs of sexual assault. No traces of alcohol in the blood. The results of screens for other drugs are still a week or so away. No ligature marks on the body."

"Do the cops know who did it yet?" I asked her mechanically.

"No suspects yet, but the cops have ruled out sexual assault and robbery. The wallet, with two hundred dollars in cash and all her credit cards, and a Rolex watch were still on the body. And her BMW coupe was in a parking area three miles away, locked and unmolested, with the alarm still on. Christ, this girl must have been richer than God."

"So what do they think?"

"At this point, they don't know. Obviously, a lot of anger was involved, you know, because of the overkill factor. The perp or perps used a lot more force than was necessary to kill her. In that case, you've got a killer who's really angry and out of control." She paused. "It'll take a while to find out who did this, Carmen. I'm sorry about your friend. Are you okay?"

"Yeah. Thanks, Terry."

I hung up. "Dear God," I said. Waves of grief, nausea and terror washed over me.

As I drove to work that day, I reviewed the circumstances of her death, careful to keep the brutality of it out of my mind. Toni went to the scene of the crime willingly. She either knew her attacker or was surprised at the scene.

I squinted at the afternoon sun as I waited for the traffic light to change.

What was she doing at Cherokee Park? Lake Sequoyah, a reservoir for the city's drinking water, was a dangerous place, especially after dark on the weekends. High school and college students gathered at the parking lots near the pumping station on the lake's south end to drink heavily, fight and paw one another. Nearly every week when the weather was warm, I read about thefts, assaults, rapes and accidental drownings in the area. Toni was found in heavy woods on the northeast end of the lake, far from the party scene.

When I got to work, I opened the directory to my personal queue and called up the file TONI, which I had created the night of her call.

I reread the notes I had taken nearly two weeks earlier:

He called me up to tell me he was going to get even with me. Like I would be scared of him. . . . I have a news tip for you. . . . I'm onto a very big story, but if I give it to you, you have to promise to protect somebody involved. . . . Sorry. I've got to go. They're leaving. I'll call you tomorrow with the details.

Why hadn't I pressed her for details? If she had confided her plan to me, I might have recognized the danger and talked her out of whatever she had done that night. And she might still be alive.

"Toni," I said aloud, "I'm so sorry."

The day after the funeral, the questioning began. Detectives took statements from all of us — Julia, Charles, Donna, Tom, Leonard and me — about Toni. I told the police everything, about the Toni's feud with Leonard, his threats against her, and the mysterious call the night she disappeared.

By the end of the week, Leonard was in jail, held on a charge of first-degree murder.

I found out through Terry that Leonard's story simply didn't hold together. He had disappeared from campus for three days — his absence overlapping with the time that Toni had disappeared. Apparently, he had simply gone camping by himself in the woods in southeastern Oklahoma so he could see the fall foliage. He offered the police no witnesses who could verify his whereabouts. He had motive, an avowed dislike of Toni and a series of disputes with her. He had left threatening messages on Toni's answering machine. A neighbor even reported seeing a man matching Leonard's description letting the air out of Toni's tires in the driveway of her town house. The cops got a warrant, searched his car, and found a bloody baseball bat in the trunk. If the hair and blood samples matched Toni's, and if he was found guilty, Leonard would probably face the death penalty, or at least a life sentence.

CHAPTER FIVE

The Sunday after Toni's funeral and Leonard's arrest, Grandma and I sat across from each other at her dining room table. She hadn't felt like cooking, so she had picked up two boxed dinners from Kentucky Fried Chicken on the way home from church. It was pointless to tell her that I preferred to avoid such grease-laden fare. She wouldn't want to hear anything about my unending battle to watch my weight and lower my cholesterol. She would have simply considered me impolite.

"How's your chicken?" she said.

"Great," I said.

"Brother Rex preached a lovely sermon today."

"That's nice," I said.

"His text was Romans six, twenty-three."

I knew the passage well. *For the wages of sin is death, but the gift of God is eternal life through Jesus Christ our Lord.*

"You remember that verse, don't you, Carmen? You haven't been away from the body of believers so long that you've forgotten it, have you?"

I put down my drumstick and looked at Grandma, who regarded me with the eyes of a prosecuting attorney.

"Yes, I remember it."

"And what do you make of it, now that Toni Stewart has departed from this world?" she said, pointing her plastic fork at me.

"I don't fucking believe this."

"Don't you dare use that language in my house," Grandma roared, slamming her hand on the table. "Don't you have any respect for me?"

"Respect?" I shouted back at her. "That's a funny word coming from you. For God's sake, I just went to Toni's funeral, and you're grilling me about her death? Don't you find that obscene?"

Grandma stood up and pointed her long, narrow index finger into my face. "That woman's death is a message to you from God on high to turn from your evil ways. I know what kind of woman she was. Homosexuality leads to death. Come back to the church, Carmen. I don't want to have to bury you in a few years."

As I walked out, she was still yelling at me. "I'm trying to save your life, Carmen. The Bible doesn't leave any room for doubt."

"Well, look what the cat refused to drag in," Julia said, looking up from a long Victorian novel. Her long, elegant body was stretched out on the sofa. "How was lunch?"

"KFC, served with a heaping order of fire and brimstone." I sat next to her on the couch. After I had filled her in on the old woman's latest outrage, I asked, "And what did you do for fun today?"

"Donna and Tom dropped by. We decided to disband the group," she said. "With Leonard behind bars and Toni dead, we just don't see a point of keeping up with it. Then Charles came back from the library. He and Donna and Tom went off to Wilde's."

"Why didn't you go?"

"They asked me, but I just didn't feel like it," Julia said. "But after they left, I got a call from Leonard." She paused to gauge my reaction. "He wants you to come see him."

I stood up. "What?" I was outraged.

Julia held up her hands to ward off my anger. "Listen, Carmen, he needs our help. He told me he didn't do it. He knows your work on the Barrett case, and he thought you might be willing to talk to him."

"He's the prime suspect in Toni's murder," I said furiously. "He has a lawyer, doesn't he?"

"Yes. A public defender. And she's trying to get him to plea bargain for life without parole. Carmen, it wouldn't hurt to just talk to him."

Ordinarily, I opposed the death penalty, but in this case, I would gladly strap Leonard in the chair, pull the switch and watch him fry. "The bastard bashed her head in with a baseball bat," I said, spitting the words. "I owe him absolutely nothing."

Julia took a breath. "I know you're upset, but please stop shouting, Carmen. Leonard hasn't been proven guilty. If he did it, he should rot in prison. The question is, if," she said. "I consider him a friend. I respect him. He's out in all his classes, and that takes a lot of courage."

"A friend? The guy is a bona fide psycho."

Julia looked at me pleadingly. "I know he's obsessive about Charles. And his behavior toward Toni certainly makes him suspect. But it wasn't totally unprovoked. Be honest. She could be very cruel where he was concerned."

"Does that mean he had the right to beat her to death?" I said vehemently. Realizing my anger was nearly out of control, I walked outside and sat down on a large rock behind our apartment. It was a cold, wet, overcast day in early November. The fall foliage had passed its peak. The trees were nearly bare now.

Julia followed. "Leonard has absolutely no social skills. He's not the most appealing person. But he grew up in a hellish environment —"

"What are you, his shrink or his den mother?" I shouted.

Julia glowered at me. "Look, I did my best to try to understand your relationship with Toni —"

"Just stop," I said. I couldn't fight anymore. Her words had broken me. I sobbed, rage and sadness spilling out of me.

"I don't want to make you feel any worse," she said, crouching beside me and putting her arms around me. "I know you miss her. I know you loved her. I know it makes you crazy that somebody took her life. It's going to take a long time to get over."

Pain and grief strangled my heart.

"Don't you owe it to her to find out for sure whether Leonard really did it?"

Unable to speak, I nodded at Julia.

Monday morning, I headed downtown. The Frontier City/County Jail occupied the top three floors of the County Courthouse in the Civic Center complex.

I parked in a hideously expensive lot next to the courthouse and headed into the main entrance. A sheriff's deputy sat behind a long table next to a metal detector.

"Excuse me," I said to the haggard, young man guarding the desk. "What is the procedure for visiting prisoners?"

"All people with business on the courthouse premises must pass through the metal detector, ma'am," he said.

"And after that?"

"Please pass through the metal detector," he said impatiently.

I walked through. "Now what?"

He pointed to his left. There sat a desk marked INFORMATION. I stood there for five minutes before a middle-aged woman with bright blue eye shadow and a lacquered red bouffant came to the desk. She shuffled papers for another three minutes before she finally acknowledged my presence.

"I'm here to visit a prisoner."

"You have to sign in," she said unpleasantly.

"Here?" I said.

"Of course not."

"Then where?"

She rolled her eyes. "Take the main bank of elevators to the third floor. The signs will guide you from there," she said, not bothering to disguise her exasperation.

Instead of calling her a bitch, which I really wanted to do, I thanked her politely.

On the third floor, I found the Prisoner Visitation Sign-In Room. The room, which could have easily been mistaken for a way station to hell, was packed with miserable souls — young women clutching scrawny toddlers with Kool-Aid stained faces, aging matrons with bad teeth and worn-out expressions, tired men wearing cheap vinyl jackets and chain-smoking Marlboro Lights. I sat at the remotest bench I could find, avoided eye contact with my desolate companions and waited for my name to be called. After the longest forty-five minutes of my life, I was led by a ghoulish-looking man who towered over me by at least a foot to the visiting area, a row of cubicles on the twelfth floor.

"Cubicle five," the deputy said. "You got fifteen minutes. I am required by law to advise you that all conversations are monitored."

I opened the door and found myself in a tiny room about the size of a phone booth. On the other side of smeared glass reinforced with metal mesh sat

Leonard, looking pale, gaunt and frightened in his orange jail jumpsuit.

Seeing him again, the wild anger I felt yesterday nearly overtook me. I took a deep breath. I was here for a reason, I reminded myself. I needed to find out whether Leonard was Toni's killer. For Toni. For Julia. And for me. To do that, I needed to stay rational.

Just as in the movies, we had to talk by telephone.

"Carmen," he said, "it's horrible in here. You have no idea. I had my bail hearing today. The judge set it at a quarter of a million dollars. That means somebody has to post twenty-five thousand dollars. My parents don't have that kind of money. They live in a trailer, for God's sake. They didn't even come to the hearing. My lawyer, Gloria Russo from the Public Defender's Office, didn't even try to get the bail lowered. She's horrible and incompetent. I haven't taken a shower since they arrested me. And they've got me in isolation because the men in here —"

I struggled to empty myself of emotion. Feel nothing, I said to myself. Think clearly. "Leonard," I said, trying to sound and feel calm, "I'm only allowed fifteen minutes. I can't do anything about the conditions here. And I can't raise bail for you. Let's not waste time talking about things I can't help you with. If you're being harassed, talk to your lawyer."

He looked at me as if he were going to cry.

"Toni was a very good friend of mine. I have to have an honest answer. Did you kill her?" I said, my voice hard. I stared at him intently, hoping this would make him tell the truth.

86

"No, I didn't." His answer was simple, but there was a look of uncertainty in his eyes.

My rage began to flare up again. I quelled it. "Did you ever threaten her?"

"No." His expression remained the same.

My hand tightened around the receiver. My voice grew severe. "Leonard, the night she disappeared, she told me you had threatened her. You also threatened her in front of a crowd of people at Wilde's."

His face became twisted. "I threatened her, but not with violence. I just wanted to let her know that if she kept fucking with me, I was going to fight back."

"And that's what you did?" I demanded.

"I flattened her tires. I didn't even slash them. I just let the air out."

Hoping to see him break, I kept after him. "What about the calls?"

He lowered his head and pulled at his long hair, which had grown greasy during his jail stint.

"You did make threatening calls, didn't you?"

He looked up at me. "I just told her to watch out, because I was going to get even. I only wanted to scare her."

"Why, Leonard?" I said, hammering at him.

"She was a slick, wealthy bitch who'd had everything handed to her," he said vehemently. "She made me look bad — in front of Charles. It made me crazy. I'm sorry." He started crying. "I've never had anything. You know? I grew up in a trailer park on the west side. My father worked in an oil refinery until he got laid off. My mother works at a hamburger joint. We never had any money. I never had any friends. The popular kids, the ones like her, always pushed me around, all the way through school. So, I finally find a group where I might fit in. And I meet this great guy, and Toni made a fool out of me."

I couldn't resist the chance to state reality as cruelly as possible. "If something was going to happen between you and Charles, Toni couldn't have stopped it," I said flatly.

Taking a moment to regroup, he rubbed his face. "A couple of nights later, she had me thrown out of Wilde's. She lied to the bartender — told him I was making trouble for her. All I did was try to talk to her."

I regarded him skeptically.

"Ask Donna," he said, slapping the table in anger, then looking around to see whether a guard would scold him for his outburst. He took a breath and tried to calm himself. "She was with me that night. Look, I know you don't like me —"

"Don't like you? Leonard, that's a severe understatement. You're charged with killing my friend. My friend," I said. This rage would never do, I told myself. I had to regain control and put him on the defensive. I took a breath and looked at my watch. Then, I resumed staring hard into his eyes. "I've invested nearly two hours of my day off to hear your story, which, so far, has been full of half-truths and outright lies. I can see why your lawyer wants you to plea bargain, because you're your own worst enemy."

He looked stunned.

"If you didn't do it, why did the cops find a bloody bat in the trunk of your car?" That's it, I told myself. Make him explain.

"I swear to God I don't know how it got there. Maybe the cops planted it." He was clearly distraught.

I kept my voice accusatory. "I find that hard to believe. Why would they want to plant evidence in the car of an innocent man?"

"I didn't kill her," he said, looking right at me and pronouncing each word slowly and distinctly. "I swear to God I didn't."

Don't let him breathe, I thought. "Then why did you leave town at the exact time Toni vanished?"

"I wanted to see the trees."

"Cut the shit. Nobody's buying that ridiculous story. A busy graduate student doesn't have time to take off in the middle of the week for a foliage tour."

"Oh God," he said, shaking his head. "I know how this looks. I knew I was getting out of control. I admit it. I was obsessing on Charles and so angry at Toni that I scared myself. So I just headed off to Beavers Bend, just to get my head together, you know?"

"Did you register for a campsite? Is there any way we could verify that you were actually out of town?" I pulled my note pad out of my jacket pocket.

"I told the cops this too. I paid a fee for a remote site, but I did it in cash. I had a receipt, but I didn't keep it."

Taking notes as Leonard spoke, I hit him with another question to keep him off balance. "Where exactly did you camp? I want names, dates, times."

"I pitched a tent in the backwoods, along the old loggers trail. I was there three days."

"How did you drive to the park? What highway did you take?" I said quickly, hoping to catch him in a lie.

He paused. "Um, U.S. Seventy-five to Henryetta. Then I took the Indian Nations Turnpike to Highway Three —"

I interrupted. "What did you do with your turnpike receipts?"

"I don't know. Oh, I think I threw them on the floor, or tucked them behind the visor or put them in the glove box. Maybe I threw them away. I don't remember."

"Those receipts, if I'm not mistaken, are stamped with the date and time, so they would confirm your story. That is, if you're telling the truth."

For the first time, his face looked hopeful. "I am, Carmen. I swear I am. Does this mean you believe me?"

His inability to read other people's feelings and reactions was stunning. Or perhaps he really was an innocent man, willing to cling to any hope that could somehow free him from this predicament. "Believe you? Not by a longshot," I said, looking over my notebook. "But your story is worth checking out."

"Thank you, Carmen," he said, offering a weak smile.

"Don't thank me," I said.

When I left, my heart was pounding. I wasn't sure I had accomplished anything.

* * * * *

After I left the jail, Terry Harris and I sat in old school desks at Nick's, a greasy eatery half a block away from the Times building. Like a snake unhinging its jaw to gulp down a giant rat, Terry took an enormous bite of the barbecued beef sandwich I had just bought her in exchange for information on the investigation of Toni's murder. I had no idea how she managed to eat so much fat-laden food and stay so thin. Her cholesterol count must have been six hundred.

"I've talked to Russo from a phone at the courthouse," I said. "Leonard says she's incompetent."

"That's bullshit. Gloria Russo is one of the best young attorneys the P.D.'s office has. She was top of her class at the University of Oklahoma," Terry said between bites.

"I gave her the information about the turnpike receipts. She said she'd check into it, but she didn't sound too enthusiastic."

Terry swallowed. "She's dealing with the scum of the earth every day of her life. Plus, she's got cases coming out the ass. I'm sure that makes her less than perky."

"So what have you heard about the case against Leonard?"

"They've given it to Morgan Henderson, also known as 'The Tiger Shark.' One sniff of blood and he's all over you. Morgan told me, off the record, that he's going to push for the death penalty unless Leonard plea bargains. And he never says that unless he's got a case that he can win. And he wins a lot of them.

"He's got eyewitnesses seeing Leonard raise holy hell with the victim all over town right before she disappears. He's got the suspect making threatening calls to her right before the murder and the tape and phone records to back that up. Plus Leonard has made contradictory statements to the police. He disappeared when the murder took place. His alibi is for shit. And if the blood on the bat turns out to be Toni's, he'll fry."

"Looks like I'll just have to wait and see," I said.

"Hey, thanks for the sandwich," she said as I headed for the door. "I'll keep you posted."

That afternoon, I stopped by to see Grandma, who gave me a chilly reception at her back door.

"Can we talk?" I said.

"I'm not feeding you," she said, opening the door to her back hallway.

We walked through the kitchen and dining room to the living room. I took a seat on the sofa while she sat in her recliner.

"This has got to stop, you know," I said.

She said nothing, staring straight ahead.

"We're not going to get anywhere by arguing religion. I know you're upset that Charles is staying with me. I know you're upset I live with Julia. I also know that you never approved of Toni, and you feel her murder is some kind of judgment from God."

She lit one of her foul-smelling little black cigars.

"I'm sorry. I love you, but I can't be around you right now — not until you agree to lay off this religious crusade of yours. You don't have to say anything. You don't have to apologize. All you have to do is stop."

She stoically puffed away at her cigar.

"It's up to you," I said. "Call me whenever you're ready. And if you need anything, I'm always here for you."

I left her sitting in a cloud of cigar smoke.

Thursday afternoon, Russo called me back. The turnpike and campsite receipts hadn't turned up in Leonard's car. None of the rangers at the state park remembered seeing Leonard. Two weeks later, the state crime lab reported the blood on the bat was Toni's. As far as I was concerned, Leonard was on his own. And I hoped he would fry.

My twenty-seventh birthday in November, Thanksgiving, Christmas, and New Year's all went by without a word from Grandma. I mailed her a Christmas card and package. She sent them back unopened. Edna Sullivan wouldn't give up this feud easily.

I still drove by her house every day and phoned up her neighbors to make sure she was all right. And I saw Mrs. Harmon, the woman from my grandmother's Sunday school class, driving by my house at least twice a week. Traveling about two miles per hour, she gawked out her car window at me. I waved and smiled whenever I saw her. I was sure she was spying for Grandma.

Meanwhile, Leonard was bound over for trial on a charge of first-degree murder. Unable to post bond, he remained behind bars. His trial was set to begin the last week of February.

It was a Tuesday night in mid-January. I glanced at the clock. Deadline was twenty minutes away. I quickly skimmed through the file assigned to me — BODY.

A badly decomposed body of a man was discovered yesterday in a heavily wooded area at Cherokee Park, the Frontier City Police Department reported today.

The remains were sent to the county coroner's office for identification, said Detective Sgt. Mel Gibbs.

Two fishermen found the remains on the west side of the park, Gibbs said.

The department would not release the names of the fishermen.

"There's not much to report at this point," Gibbs said. "We won't know more until the coroner gets back to us."

I quickly wrote a headline: BODY FOUND IN CHEROKEE PARK. It wasn't very exciting, but unedited stories were backing up, and deadline was growing closer by the minute.

"Carmen, what are you doing with that story?"

Newman said loud enough so everyone in the newsroom could hear his high, whiny voice. "Don't you know what time it is? We have a deadline, you know."

"Yes, Jerry. I've known how to tell time since kindergarten. I just signed off on the story."

As I sullenly glared at Newman, I realized how thoroughly I despised him. A fantasy emerged. I would walk over, smack him across the face, and then curse him out in front of everyone, leaving no insult unhurled. After I had unloaded all of my rage and contempt, he would melt, just as the Wicked Witch of the West had in The Wizard of Oz. Triumphant, I would lead the entire copy desk in a rousing version of "Ding Dong, the Witch is Dead."

I smiled evilly and started work on the next story.

Wednesday, on the way to my desk, I passed by Terry Harris's work station. She was frantically typing, so I didn't greet her.

"So, what did you make of that body story?" she said without looking up at me. "You know, the one they found at Lake Sequoyah. There might be a connection to the Stewart case."

"It didn't say that in the story last night."

"Read the update," she said curtly. "It just moved on the state wire about a half-hour ago."

I sat down at the nearest empty terminal and logged on.

The update was pretty much a rehash of last

night's story, except for a few new facts. The body had been found under a tarpaulin and some brush. And the skull had been crushed.

Over the next few days, information trickled in about the Lake Sequoyah remains. The victim, a five-foot-seven white male in his early twenties with black hair, had been killed by a blow to the head. No identification had been found on the body. It was estimated that the young man had been dead about two to three months. He was found wearing summer-weight clothing — khaki slacks, a pink, white, yellow and green plaid Oxford shirt and brown leather deck shoes. If investigators had further information, they weren't sharing it with the press.

"Carmen, have you found anything?" Leonard Martin demanded as soon as I picked up the phone.

It was Sunday evening, and the phone was ringing when Julia and I returned from dinner at a nearby diner.

I had long ago concluded Leonard killed Toni. My wild rage against him had subsided into a cold hatred. The matter was now in the hands of the justice system, which was almost certain to convict him. I wanted nothing more to do with him.

"No," I said calmly. "You'll have to speak to your lawyer."

"I'm only allowed five minutes. I go to trial at the end of February. That's only a little over a month away. I'm almost certain to be convicted, unless something turns up."

I said nothing, resisting the urge to tell him how glad I was that he was facing, at best, the rest of his life behind bars.

"Anyway, I have a lead you might be able to work on. I drive a VW bug. You can only open the trunk by releasing a latch from inside, not with a key from outside. I never lock it. Anybody who wanted could have popped open the trunk. I told my lawyer that my car should be dusted for prints so maybe we could find whoever planted the bat," he said, his voice fast and frantic, as if he could wear me down with the sheer number of words that poured out of his mouth.

"And what did she say?" I said, my impatience mounting.

"She said the car had already been dusted when it was impounded and that the police hadn't found anything significant." He paused, waiting for me to answer.

"I can't help you," I said flatly.

"Carmen, don't you see? My lawyer thinks she's going to lose the case. She's still trying to get me to cut a deal."

"If you listen to the inmates, America's prisons are filled with innocent men and women." My head was pounding from the sound of his voice.

"I *am* innocent," he shrieked. He took a moment to compose himself. "The person who planted the bat had to be close enough to me and Toni to know we were fighting. That's how they framed me. You've just got to help me. You said you would."

My resentment nearly exploded. "You didn't hire

me as a private investigator. And I have absolutely no obligation —"

Oblivious, Leonard went on, "For the record, they didn't find my prints on that bat. If I was stupid enough to tote the murder weapon around in the trunk of my car, why was I smart enough to wear gloves or wipe it down?"

I didn't reply.

"If you don't help me, nobody will. Just think about it, Carmen," he said, his voice pleading, demanding, maddeningly insisting that I intervene.

After I hung up, I sat next to Julia on the sofa and filled her in on my conversation.

Suddenly and sharply, I realized I might have been all wrong about the case. "For the first time, I'm beginning to have serious doubts about Leonard's guilt," I said.

The notion of Leonard's potential innocence was infuriating. I had treated him terribly. That would made me a jerk. Worse still, Toni's killer would be on the loose.

"There's something here that doesn't fit — namely the second body," I said. "I could believe in a heartbeat that Leonard was crazy enough to kill Toni, but this other guy? What's the motive? If he was out on a killing rampage, Charles would have been the most likely victim. Plus there's the bloody bat in his unlocked VW. It's free of prints, right? Somebody who wipes off prints is going to be smart enough to get rid of the bat."

"Or frame somebody with it," Julia added.

"Exactly."

"So what are we going to do?" she asked.

"Well, I'm going to start digging around some more," I said. "Wake me up before you leave for class tomorrow. I'm going to Oklahoma City to talk to Toni's mother."

CHAPTER SIX

I pulled up in the circular drive in front of the Stewarts' house, a sprawling two-story stone house surrounded by a landscaped pine grove.

I parked my Honda Civic behind a black BMW sedan and headed up the stone walkway.

The door chimes played a theme from a Tchaikovsky piano concerto as I waited for the heavy carved front door to open. Mrs. Stewart, looking stoically elegant in a black pantsuit and white silk blouse, met me. When I called that morning, she had seemed eager for me to visit, happy to hear from anyone who had been close to her daughter.

I handed her a budget bouquet of daisies I had picked up in Frontier City and swaddled in wet paper towels before hitting the road. "My condolences."

"Thank you. How nice to see you again," she said blankly as she led me into the foyer. "Let me take your coat, dear." She carefully hung up my parka, which I had had for ten years, in a closet in the entryway.

I followed her into the cavernous family room, which was warmed by a fire blazing in the massive rough stone fireplace. Overlooking the room was an elk head, stuffed and mounted over the mantel. I couldn't help but stare.

"My husband shot it on a hunting trip in Canada," Mrs. Stewart said. "He's very proud of it."

"I see," I said.

"Make yourself comfortable, dear," she said quietly. "I'll just put these in some water."

While she disappeared into the kitchen, I walked around the room, a room that showed two warring decorating sensibilities. On the wall opposite the fireplace was a glass and cherry cabinet holding at least twenty guns — shotguns, rifles, pistols. Presumably, one of these weapons brought down Mr. Elk. Next to the gun cabinet stood a high long table, also made of cherry wood. On it were displayed a porcelain ballerina on point, an ornate heart-shaped silver box, a ceramic egg painted in spring pastels and a crystal horse. Forever attracted by gewgaws, I picked up the heart-shaped box, which fit easily into the palm of my hand. I lifted the lid. It was a music box. Within a few notes, I recognized "Edelweiss." I lifted up the egg, which was silent. I wound it up, and it played "Easter Parade." I carefully replaced the music boxes and walked to the baby grand piano across the room. Sheet music for a complicated Chopin piece was unfolded on the stand of the piano, which sat next to French doors overlooking a patio and a landscaped back yard, complete with swimming pool, now covered for the winter.

I returned to the warmth of the fireplace. Photographs of Paul and Mr. Stewart dominated the left side of the mantel. These photos showed the two engaged in sports — fishing, playing catch, shooting arrows and golfing. On the right were photos of Toni — snuggling with Bradley, playing softball and soccer, graduating from high school and from college, posing next to her new BMW, complete with red ribbon on the top, holding up a sports trophy. The rest were shots of Mr. and Mrs. Stewart in various stages of their marriage and poses of Toni and Paul together.

Just then, Mrs. Stewart returned from the kitchen with the flowers, now in a crystal vase. She placed them on a cherry bookcase next to the wall, which was paneled in dark oak.

"May I offer you something to drink, dear?"

"Please don't go to any trouble, Mrs. Stewart."

"No trouble at all. The coffee should be nearly ready."

I was looking at the photos of Toni and her brother when Mrs. Stewart returned. She pushed a chrome-and-glass cart bearing coffee, cream and sugar, and two large mugs on its top rack.

Underneath was an attractively arranged platter of cookies and pastries. She was obviously a woman who knew how to entertain.

I sat down in an overstuffed dark brown leather armchair of contemporary design. The chair was so huge it nearly swallowed me. Across from me on a matching sofa sat Mrs. Stewart. I poured coffee and self-consciously added three sugars and a healthy dollop of cream. It was strong — just the way I liked it.

"Are you the musician?" I asked, launching the conversation in a non-threatening manner.

"Yes. The only one in the house."

"That Chopin piece looks very difficult," I said.

"It's challenging," she said. "Do you play?"

"I played the violin as a kid. Later, I took up the guitar," I said. I had inherited my mother's violin. Though I had practiced relentlessly, I was never as good as I wanted to be. Stubbornly, I played all the way through school, from fifth grade to the first semester of college. I had hoped that through sheer force of will, I could transform myself into Isaac Stern. It didn't work.

"Who was your teacher?" Mrs. Stewart asked.

"I learned at school. I didn't have a private teacher. And I'm self-taught on guitar." We couldn't afford private violin lessons although I wanted them desperately. The guitar had come from a garage sale. Grandma had bought it for me for ten bucks when I was fifteen years old. I omitted these details in front of a woman who had probably spent more on her tea trolley than I did on a month's rent.

"Paul wanted nothing to do with the piano. Toni

loved playing as a little girl, but by the time she turned thirteen, we fought constantly over lessons and practice time. So she quit — over my objections."

How typical of Toni to squander her talent. I pointed to the mantel. "So how is Paul these days?"

"He's in his sophomore year at FCU. He's very active in Sigma Alpha Sigma, just like his father. He's become a fine young man. And Toni had so much to do with it. She always looked out for him, played with him. They were inseparable. I think of them in the summers — racing in the pool. Toni would always let him win when he was little. And she would spend hours with him, throwing a baseball, kicking a soccer ball with him." Her voice trailed off.

I smiled, allowing her to enjoy a pleasant memory of her children. And I made a mental note to track down Paul. But now, it was time to confront the hard facts. "Mrs. Stewart," I began carefully, "I'm not just a friend of Toni's. I am also a journalist."

She looked at me, her calm demeanor undisturbed.

"Yes."

"I've been keeping tabs on the case through my work at *The Frontier City Times*. I'm not sure Leonard Martin is responsible for Toni's . . ." I cut myself off. I didn't want to use the word "murder" in front of Mrs. Stewart. It was bad enough that her daughter was dead. I didn't want her to have to think about the savagery of the crime. "I'm not sure Leonard is guilty. I'm looking for information to make sure that police have locked up the right man." I didn't want to tell Mrs. Stewart that I was looking into the case on Leonard's behalf, for fear that she might turn against me.

"If it's money you want, you'll have to speak to my husband."

"No, Mrs. Stewart, I'm not looking for money. I just want to see this case solved, because Toni was a friend."

"I don't know."

"I can understand why you would be wary, but believe me, I just want to see the truth come out."

She nodded at me.

"Did Toni mention her dispute with Leonard before she was — before the attack?"

"She never mentioned him to me at all."

"So you weren't aware of their conflict?"

"Only after her —" She began to tear up, then composed herself. "She mentioned it to Paul. But you know Toni — she didn't take it seriously." She smiled weakly.

"Did Toni have any other enemies, as far as you were aware?"

"Oh no. Not at all. She was a lovely, popular girl."

"What about her relationship with Bradley? Any evidence of abuse?" Aside from Leonard, Bradley was the most likely suspect in Toni's death. Statistics show that when a woman shows up dead, her boyfriend or husband sent her to her grave.

"No. Not at all. Bradley was a complete gentleman with her," she said calmly.

"You know, the police found another body near where they found Toni. They haven't identified him yet. He was killed in the same way at approximately the same time, although they haven't pinpointed the time of death. He was a five-foot-seven, white, early twenties, black hair. Does that sound like anyone that Toni was spending time with?"

"The police also asked me about him. She really didn't tell me that much about her life, to be honest. She mentioned people who were important to her. If she did know this boy, she never mentioned him to me."

"I wasn't in contact with her from graduation until last fall, and I was hoping you could help me fill in the blanks."

Mrs. Stewart nodded.

"What did she do after she graduated?"

"She worked for her father at SoonerBank for a while."

"And after that?"

"She traveled, dabbled in various things." Mrs. Stewart stared at the fireplace. Her eyes welled up with tears.

"Toni mentioned to me that she lived in San Francisco for a while, right before coming to law school. What was she doing there?"

Mrs. Stewart shifted uncomfortably on the sofa. "Well, she was working at a bookstore," she said as she stared at the fireplace. Only the tears rolling down her face revealed her deep sadness.

"Mrs. Stewart, are you all right?"

"Oh, my dear, if you only knew. We always knew Toni was free-spirited and, frankly, quite tomboyish. After graduation, we thought she would settle down, marry Bradley — you know, follow a normal track. But she seemed to have no direction. After she quit the bank, she took a minimum-wage job at a video store. She talked about backpacking across Europe. She broke up with Bradley. After a year of this, David, that's my husband, finally got fed up. He thought she was drifting. He was trying to get Toni to pull herself together."

Mrs. Stewart began weeping bitterly, her elegant facade stripped away. Unable to speak for a while, she wiped her nose on a napkin from the coffee tray and then swept back a strand of graying hair that had fallen into her face.

"I'm sorry to make such a scene in front of you."

"That's all right," I said. "You're dealing with a lot right now."

"One evening, over dinner, he told her to make something of her life or get out. She left that night in a rage. David wouldn't even let her take the car, which I had bought for her. Toni was so stubborn. An ultimatum was the worst thing for her."

Mrs. Stewart shook her head regretfully. Suddenly, her face turned angry. "I set up trust funds for Toni and Paul with Daddy's money, you see. He left all of us quite a bit when he passed away several years ago. David forced me to cut off her fund."

I swallowed my disgust. I found something despicable about a woman who let a man bully her.

"We didn't see her for a while. She lived with friends, drifted around, did odd jobs. David keeps me on an allowance, and he watches every penny. But I used the money Daddy left me," Mrs. Stewart said, her elegant face calmly defiant. "Toni was my girl. No one could make me abandon her. God only knows where she was most of the time. But I sent her money whenever she asked."

So Mrs. Stewart wasn't the dish rag I thought she was. I made a mental note to stop making snap judgments.

"About a year ago, I got a call from San Francisco. Toni had a bohemian living arrangement out there, with a bunch of women, all in one house. She said she was happy and asked me to come out to see her. I even had to lie to David. I told him I was going to a sorority reunion. Well, when I got out there, I was appalled. I pleaded with her to come back home and make something of herself. But she wouldn't listen to me. Then, a few months later, she called me up and said she wanted to come back. I could tell that she was at a low ebb, but I didn't push her to tell me why. She asked me to approach her father. Of course, I did. At first, David was dead set against her return. We fought terribly. I really thought it would destroy our marriage." She paused. "I guess I shouldn't be telling you these things."

"No really," I said, "it's all right."

Mrs. Stewart walked to the French doors. The sky was steely gray outside. "He put very strict conditions on Toni's return to the family," she said, looking outside, her voice far away. I had the feeling she was talking more to herself than me. "When Toni got back, he was very harsh with her. She was an emotional wreck. He insisted that she pull her life together. David pushed her to start seeing Bradley again. He was absolutely adamant about it. I didn't think it was a good idea to force things between them, but he doesn't listen to me when he's like that." Mrs. Stewart covered her eyes, as if to block out the memory.

"That must be very hard for you," I said, not knowing what else to say.

"Toni started seeing Bradley again and enrolled in law school. She and Bradley announced their engagement. Her father was satisfied. I persuaded him that we should buy the town house. He went along, because it was a good investment. But I wanted her to be independent."

"You did an excellent job, Mrs. Stewart," I said. "Toni was always her own woman."

"Thank you. That's good to hear." She turned around and smiled at me with tears in her eyes. "Is there anything else you need?"

"I'd like to contact the people Toni was living with in San Francisco, if you can give me their names. I'd like the name of the bookstore where she worked. I also need current addresses and phone numbers for Paul and Bradley."

"Certainly," she said.

While Mrs. Stewart searched for the information I needed in another room, I returned to the cherry wood table with the music box collection. I had just picked up the crystal horse when Mrs. Stewart came back into the room.

"All of those were gifts from Toni," she said. "She got me hooked on music boxes."

"This is a side of Toni I never saw."

"Toni had a way of keeping most people at a distance. Even her father, I'm afraid. She didn't like to appear vulnerable."

Tears filled my eyes. "Thanks for everything, Mrs. Stewart."

"Please, dear, call me Louise. And if you need

anything else, just let me know. And call me as soon as you find out anything about this case. Just be sure to call during the day, while David is at work. I'm afraid he can be a bully, and I'm not sure he would be polite to you. You see, he didn't always approve of Toni's friendships."

I looked at her. I was certain that Mrs. Stewart, in her own diplomatic way, was telling me that her husband hated my guts. "I'll keep you posted."

"Please take one of the music boxes," she said.

"Are you sure?"

"Yes, I insist. Toni cared very deeply for you, in her own way. When she used to call me from school, she talked about you more than she talked about Bradley."

I blushed.

"I'm sure she would have wanted you to have one."

"Thank you. I'll treasure it." I picked up the heart-shaped box and left.

By the time I got home after my visit with Mrs. Stewart, it was early afternoon, and a cold front had moved through. A bitter northwest wind tore through me as I stepped out of my car.

Once inside my apartment, I brewed coffee to warm me up and went over the list Mrs. Stewart had given me. She had supplied me with Paul's and Bradley's numbers but none of Toni's San Francisco housemates' names. The only name she had given me from Toni's days out west was "Woman's Eye Books — Faith Brooks."

"Well, I'll be damned," I said aloud. Judging from the name, it was a sure bet that Toni had worked at a lesbian bookstore.

Despite Mrs. Stewart's advice to avoid her husband, I called SoonerBank's corporate headquarters in Oklahoma City. Mr. Stewart would be in meetings all that afternoon, his secretary, a Miss Monica Davis, assured me. I insisted that she tell him that I was a friend of Toni's and that he call me back as soon as possible. Then I called the bookstore.

Much to my surprise, Faith Brooks herself answered.

"Hi, Faith. I'm calling from Frontier City, Oklahoma. My name is Carmen Ramirez. I'm a friend of Antoinette Stewart. Were you her supervisor?"

"We're a women's collective. We don't use terms like 'supervisor.' "

"But you worked with Toni?"

"She worked at the store for several months. Did she put me down as a reference?"

"Oh no. I got your name from her mother."

"I met Mrs. Stewart when she visited our house. She's a very nice woman."

"You lived with Toni?"

"What's this all about?" she said, her voice increasingly wary.

"Oh, I'm sorry. I guess this call must sound strange. I'm trying to track down some information on Toni's life while she was in San Francisco."

"What on earth for?"

Suddenly, it occurred to me that her friends there hadn't heard the news. "Brace yourself. I have some bad news. Toni was murdered."

Faith dropped the phone and screamed.

"Faith, please, pick up," I said. On the other end, I heard wild sobbing.

"This is Katie Vance. Who is this?" an angry voice said. "What the hell is going on?"

I filled Katie in on my reason for calling.

"Oh holy shit," Katie said. "Give me your number. I'll call you back."

Two hours later, Katie Vance returned my call.

"Faith's friends are looking after her right now," she said.

"She took it very hard."

"What do you expect? Faith and Toni were lovers."

A surge of jealousy raced through me. I paused until it was under control. "Oh, my God. I didn't know. I'm so sorry."

"I've only been in the city three months. I've been at the store for two months, but I've heard all about Toni. She hit town, got a job here, and within a few weeks, she and Faith were hot and heavy. Faith has been a wreck ever since Toni split."

"Do you know why they broke up?"

"Not for certain."

"Do you know whether anybody out your way would have been angry enough to track her down in Oklahoma?"

"As far as I knew, the only person here who had any reason to hold a grudge against Toni is Faith. They parted on bad terms. I heard that Toni cheated on Faith. I know for sure that Faith was really hurt. But she is the gentlest woman I know. The bookstore is infested with mice, and she won't use spring traps or poison. She puts out non-lethal traps and releases the mice outside. Of course, they come back. Does that sound like a killer to you?"

"Can you ask around and see if she crossed anybody else? Toni slept with men and women. Maybe there's an angry ex-boyfriend floating around out there."

"I'll see what I can find out."

"Also, I need Faith's home number."

"I don't think that's a good idea."

"Katie, I won't harass her. I just want to make sure that Toni's killer is brought to justice."

"Listen, I'll give her your number, and if she wants to call you back, she can."

"Thanks." I hung up.

Katie was out to shield Faith from my questions, and I didn't blame her for it. I would probably never hear back from Faith and I didn't want to be forced to nag her at the bookstore. I called directory assistance. Brooks' number was listed. I would give her a few days to recover from the shock, then call again.

Somewhere inside I was happy. At least Toni had found the courage to experience the love of a woman, even if I wasn't that woman.

Tuesday, before going in for the late shift at the paper, I called SoonerBank again.

"Miss Ramirez, Mr. Stewart has a busy schedule. He will call you at his earliest convenience," Miss Monica Davis said sternly.

"Miss Davis, I will keep calling until I get through. Please tell him I need to speak with him. This is an urgent matter. I promise I won't take up much of his time."

"Very well," she said.

After I listened to Musak versions of "Strawberry Fields" and "Dreamboat Annie," the secretary came back on the line. "Mr. Stewart is out of the office for the rest of the afternoon," she said.

"And it took you five minutes to figure that out? I'm not buying that. He's sitting there in his office. He just doesn't want to talk to me."

"Good day, Miss Ramirez." With that, she hung up.

After talking to the secretary, I headed over to Bradley Pennington's apartment, which was on the FCU campus. I had phoned him that morning and told him I'd like to make a condolence call. He seemed genuinely moved and told me to stop by between two and three that afternoon.

A lanky man with shoulder-length greasy brown hair met me at the door of Bradley Pennington's apartment. He wore a faded pink Hawaiian shirt and filthy jeans. His eyes were small, red slits. The sweet, pungent smell of marijuana smoke hit my nostrils. "Is Bradley in?" I asked.

"Who wants to know?"

"I'm Carmen Ramirez. He's expecting me."

Pothead closed the door partially. "Brad, some chick with a foreign name wants to talk to you." He reopened the door. "Wait out here. He's in the shower. I'd invite you in, but the place is a fucking dump."

As I waited, I stamped my feet to keep them from freezing. At least the wall blocked the blasting north wind. Still, I was bitterly cold — and even more uneasy. Meeting Bradley again after all these years would be tough. When he came over for weekend visits with Toni, I made myself scarce. The few times I actually ran into him, he was pleasant enough, but I resented him anyway. Back then, I pretended he didn't exist so I could delude myself into believing that Toni belonged to me.

Now, we were no longer rivals. Bradley was, quite simply, a suspect. One with a classic motive — jealousy. All the signs were there, if he could read them. His girlfriend was restless, perhaps ready to abandon heterosexuality. She had had a woman lover. She was attending Julia's group. She had made a pass at me. Even if he didn't know the particulars, Bradley may have sensed that Toni had a roving eye. And there was the young man found near Toni. Perhaps they has been sexually involved. Any of these factors could have driven Bradley to kill. He was close enough to Toni to know about her conflict with Leonard. Bradley, I reasoned, could have framed Leonard.

But Bradley might well be innocent. How could I question a person who had just lost the woman he loved, especially when I told him I was coming by on a condolence call? Did I only suspect him because I had once been so jealous of him?

"Hi," Bradley said. His short black hair was still damp from the shower. One look at his eyes, which were dark brown, told me he hadn't been indulging in marijuana along with his roommate. Wearing a crisp, white shirt and pressed jeans, he presented a neat, handsome appearance. A large man, he towered over me by a full eight inches.

"Hi," I said, shaking his hand, which was damp. "Is there someplace we can talk privately?"

"Sure. But I have something to do at three. I gotta be back by then." Bradley grabbed a green army overcoat. "Would you mind going with me to the laundry room? I have to check on my stuff."

"Sure," I said, following him to the basement. The room was deserted, except for us. At least it was warm, if bleak. For some reason, I had always found laundry rooms depressing. I watched him transfer a load of wet jeans from the washer to the dryer before I spoke. "So," I said, "how does a law student wind up with a heavy duty pothead like that for a roommate?"

"You'll have to excuse Jackson. He's incredible, isn't he? I'm trying to switch out of this place next semester. Believe it or not, he's working on an M.F.A. in art. And he makes excellent grades. His paintings are highly thought of by the faculty. How he can even function like that is beyond me."

"I'm really sorry about Toni," I said after a moment of strained silence. "It must be quite a loss for you. I meant to speak to you at the funeral, but I just couldn't."

"Louise told me you'd come. It meant a lot to her. I really wasn't registering much of anything that day." He plugged in two quarters and set the dryer to "cotton/heavy duty."

"So, how are you holding up?"

"Oh, you know, law school gives me something to focus on. I try not to think much — just stay busy."

"Mrs. Stewart told me that you two were going to be married this summer."

"That was the plan." He measured out some bleach and poured it into a washer with a trembling hand.

"Bradley, what do you think about the case against Leonard Martin?"

"I really can't bear to think about it right now. It's all I can do to just get out of bed, go to class, and function like a human being."

"I don't want to upset you, but I think that the police may have arrested the wrong person for Toni's murder. I'm trying to look for things they might have missed." I gave him what I hoped was a reassuring smile.

"What can you do that the police can't?" he said as he loaded whites into the washer.

"With Leonard behind bars, they're not looking for the actual killer anymore."

Bradley looked down at his blue plastic laundry basket. "You're wasting your time."

"That may well be, but it's my time."

He looked at me blankly.

"Do you know how many people she told about her conflict with Leonard?"

He shook his head and answered easily. "No, I don't."

"Did she discuss it with you?"

"Yes, briefly," he said calmly. "She didn't make a big deal out of it."

"The police found another body close to where Toni was found. He was killed the same way and around the same time. A white guy in his early twenties, five-seven, black hair. Does that sound like any of Toni's friends?"

Bradley sighed. His patience must have been running thin. "The police asked me the same thing. I've never heard of him."

"Toni hung around with a lot of different people. Are you sure that description doesn't ring a bell?"

"If I knew, I'd go to the cops."

I studied his expression. He seemed haggard and annoyed but not deceitful. "Do you know why she left San Francisco suddenly? I'm looking for anything that might be out of the ordinary. Maybe she made an enemy who tracked her back to Oklahoma."

"That's a bit of a stretch, don't you think?" he said, exasperation creeping into his voice. "Anyway, we weren't in contact while she was out West."

"Didn't she talk about it when she got back?"

"Look, I gotta get this stuff done," he said, politely but firmly trying to cut me off. He stalked over to the dryer and fiddled around with his load of jeans.

I pushed on. "Anything at all you remember might help."

"I don't know anything about it," he said. "She got tired of being there for some reason or another and she came back. What's the big deal?" His tone was defensive.

Had Toni hidden her relationship with Faith from

him? Had he figured it out on his own? "Did she tell you about Faith Brooks?"

"I'd like to know what the hell you're implying." His politeness was gone. He was clearly angry.

Using my calmest voice, I said: "Toni was living and working with Faith. Mrs. Stewart said that she was happy out there, and Toni told me the same thing. It seems unusual that she'd pick up and leave if she was happy."

"You seem to know a hell of a lot more about it than I do," he snapped.

"I wasn't even speaking to her then."

"So how come you two stopped being friends?" His eyes were narrow and cruel. "You wanted my girlfriend, didn't you? And don't try to play innocent. I know all about your relationship with her. You were in love with her. You're nothing but a dyke, and don't deny it."

His words stung. "Yes, I'm a lesbian. That's nothing to apologize for."

He took two steps toward me, his stance intimidating. My pulse responded immediately. Pleading with him and trying to explain my relationship with Toni would probably only make him furious. He was bigger than me and his anger would make him a lot stronger. I had to get away. Over the din of the dryer, no one would hear me scream for help. And running was out of the question. He stood between me and the door. I glanced back toward the row of washers. His capless bottle of bleach was resting on an empty washer. Calmly and deliberately, I moved backwards toward the bottle while maintaining eye contact with Bradley. Warn him, I told myself, then throw it in his face if he doesn't back off.

Just then, another student entered the laundry room.

"Hey, Brad, how's it going?" she said.

I didn't stick around for the reply. I sprinted to my car, locked the door and drove away like hell.

I was a few blocks away when I decided that it might prove interesting to see what Bradley was going to do at three. I turned around and parked behind a dumpster in the lot next to the Third Street United Methodist Church, a seventy-year-old structure that sat on the outer edge of the FCU campus. As a student, I'd spent many raucous nights partying with my fellow students from the Progressive Students Coalition five stories up on the roof of the classroom wing behind the gothic-style sanctuary. I was two flights up when I remembered that I had a pair of binoculars in my glove box, left there two months ago after Julia and I had attended a football game between FCU's doormat of a team and the perennial powerhouse Oklahoma Sooners. I ran back, grabbed the binoculars and raced back up the fire escape. The top story had to be reached by an old iron ladder. Keeping my eyes up, I climbed to the last story. It wasn't hard. I had made the trip many times, and my leather gloves made my grip sure. From the litter of beer, wine and whiskey containers on the roof, I could see that students were still using the roof as we had. For a moment, I felt a stab of guilt for profaning the precincts of the church all those years ago. An act of penance was in order. I rounded up all the stray bottles and cans and placed them in a brown bag I found on the roof. Positioning myself over the dumpster, I let the bag fall. Right on target, the bag fell into the dumpster.

I decided to station myself on the south wall, overlooking Third Street. The church roof offered an excellent view of the northern section of the campus. The Student Union and Business Administration buildings stood directly across from me. The law school was to the east. And the complex of student apartments where Bradley and Mr. Cannabis lived was below to the northeast. The sorority houses stood behind the apartments. Across a vast expanse of athletic fields were the frat houses. I checked my watch — two forty-five. Only fifteen more minutes in this bitter wind and I could get back to my car. I tightened the drawstring around my hood and then focused my binoculars on Bradley's apartment.

Within five minutes, Bradley walked back to his apartment with a basket of laundry. Ten minutes later, Bradley and Jackson walked out of the apartment and got on a motorcycle. With Bradley driving, they rode off toward College Street.

I rushed for the ladder. I looked down. I had always made this descent in the dark before, and I was probably a little loopy when I did it.

This time, it didn't look so easy.

The ground was a hell of a long way down. And climbing that narrow ladder seemed like a damned stupid thing to do.

"You've done it a zillion times," I reminded myself. A huge gust of wind blew out of the north. "Fuck this shit." I felt like an idiot. Five stories up,

I was trespassing in broad daylight, and worse still, I was stuck.

I stuffed the binoculars into a pocket, grabbed the loops extending from the top of the ladder, planted both hiking boots on the top rung, and ever so deliberately, swung around to face the wall. After I slowly made my way down the ladder, I sprinted down the four flights of stairs, jumped in my car and speeded toward College.

Guessing that they had headed south, I caught up with them at the intersection of College and Eleventh, where they turned west.

The motorcycle dodged easily through the heavy traffic, but luck was with me, because the lights turned red just as Bradley seemed on the verge of breaking away from me.

At Seneca, Bradley turned left and a few blocks later, he turned west again, on Fourteenth Street.

At River Drive, which runs along the east bank of the Arkansas River, they headed north. Finally, they stopped at Murray Park, overlooking the river and standing in the shadow of downtown's skyscrapers. The park should have been a pleasant, wooded remnant of the area's pre-urban days, before state-hood and white settlement, back when it had belonged to the Creek Nation. But these days, this plot of land was a crime-infested war zone that anyone with money had long since deserted. The city government and the police — not caring about the poor people who lived in the decaying housing that surrounded the park — allowed drug dealers, addicts, winos, vandals and teenage thugs to overrun the place.

I pulled into a parking space in a lot near the

desolate playground, full of broken swings, graffiti-covered slides, shattered liquor bottles, and empty McDonald's bags. Bradley and Jackson parked on the street, below my vantage point. They got off the bike and sat on a bench for about five minutes. Then a late-model black Ford pickup with tinted windows approached, heralded by the ear-destroying heavy metal pumping from inside. Bradley and Jackson walked up to the truck. There was a quick exchange. After handing something to the driver, they left with a small paper bag.

It was obvious what they were up to.

Wednesday, I drove to Oklahoma City to see Toni's father. Eschewing my usual Levis and sweater, I dressed in dark wool slacks, silk blouse, and a blazer Julia had given me for Christmas to appease his banker's sensibilities.

Oklahoma City is a flat cattle town sent into booming growth by the oil industry. Drilling rigs are everywhere, even on the lawns of the Capitol and the governor's mansion.

SoonerBank Tower, in the heart of Oklahoma City, was a twenty-story glass and steel structure lacking any human warmth. I found Mr. Stewart's name on the directory and headed up to his office on the eighteenth floor.

Miss Davis, a brunette in her late twenties, was less than pleased to see me. I would have described her as pretty if she had not been shooting murderous daggers at me with her black eyes. "Miss Ramirez, you cannot see Mr. Stewart without an appointment."

"Please tell him I'm here."

"Miss Ramirez —"

"I'm not leaving until I see him."

"Then I'll call security and have you removed," the secretary said matter-of-factly.

"I would have to make a scene, and I'm sure Mr. Stewart wouldn't like that."

She glowered at me, then picked up the phone. "Mr. Stewart, Miss Ramirez is here, and she says she won't leave unless you see her."

David Stewart, grim and imposing in his double-breasted navy pinstriped suit, opened the heavy wooden door to his office. "Come in," he said.

I walked in and he shut the door. The room was a large corner office with an impressive view of the city. Mr. Stewart sat behind his massive maple desk. Hunting photos and banking awards lined the walls behind his desk. Curiously, he had no photos of his wife or children in his office.

"I'm sorry to have to barge in on you like this, Mr. Stewart. First of all, I want to offer you my condolences."

"You have five minutes," he said icily. "Get on with it."

"I'm a journalist, and I'm looking into Toni's death. As you probably know, another victim was found in the same area. A five-foot-seven white man in his early twenties with black hair. Does that sound like any of Toni's friends?"

He glared at me with his cold gray eyes and laced his fingers together. "My daughter didn't tell me about her personal life, doubtless because she knew I wouldn't have approved of the trash she associated with."

I knew he was talking about me. "Does that include Bradley?"

He said nothing.

"Have you ever witnessed any trouble between them or any sign that Bradley abused her? Have you ever suspected Bradley of being involved with criminal activity?"

He paused, narrowing his eyes. "My daughter was never, ever abused by Bradley. I wouldn't tolerate anything of the kind. And he certainly would never be involved in any illegal activity. I'm sure you are aware that this state has laws against slander."

"Mr. Stewart, I have no interest in smearing Toni's fiancé. He's up to something that may well be illegal. I saw it with my own eyes."

"I don't know what on earth you're alluding to. Perhaps your unnatural fixation on Toni has led you to hallucinate that Bradley is a criminal."

"Unnatural fixation? I'm interested in the truth and seeing that justice is done. That's all."

"Must I spell it out? I am fully aware that you and my daughter had a lesbian attachment." He spat out the word lesbian as if he had swallowed battery acid.

My face stinging with humiliation, I said nothing.

"Now, Miss Ramirez, I must ask you to leave at once or I will have to call the police."

As I reached the door, I turned around to look at him, his face filled with contempt for me. I wished I could think of something to say to retaliate for the insults he had heaped on me, but I was paralyzed by my anger.

"Leave me and my family alone," he said angrily. "Let my daughter rest in peace."

* * * * *

That afternoon, when I got back, I checked my answering machine.

"Leave me alone, you fucking dyke. If you spy on me again, I'll show you what real harassment is all about," said an angry male voice that sounded a lot like Bradley Pennington's.

Mr. Stewart must have let Bradley know that I had followed them.

It was time to play hardball with Bradley Pennington.

CHAPTER SEVEN

That afternoon at work, I called Detective Mel Gibbs of homicide, who was quoted in the story about the remains found at Lake Sequoyah. Terry had been too busy to phone him herself. She was working on a big story — the mayor's son had been nabbed in a drug bust and she was looking forward to front-page play for the next several weeks. But she warned me that Gibbs was evasive, patronizing and self-serving.

"So, Miss Ramirez, are you on the cop beat now?" Gibbs asked.

"No, I'm an editor. I just had a couple of questions regarding the body found at Lake Sequoyah last week. Have you found any connection between his murder and the murder of Antoinette Stewart?"

"We're not ready to comment on that now."

"Off the record?"

"Sorry, little lady. No comment."

Little lady? This guy was a prince. "Toni's friends and family have been questioned about whether she knew this guy."

"And?"

"Both victims had crushed skulls."

"Do you know how many homicides we have like that?"

"How many unconnected homicides do you have where the victims are dumped at the same spot?"

"I told you already — I'm not going to comment on any possible connection between these two cases." His tone was icy.

"Detective Gibbs, are the police looking into the possibility that the weapon used in the Stewart murder was planted in Leonard's car?"

"We checked it out. No basis in fact."

"But the bat didn't have Martin's fingerprints on it, did it?"

"Where did you hear that?" he demanded.

"Now it's my turn to say no comment," I said. "Why would Leonard Martin tote the murder weapon around in the trunk of his car but make sure it was free of prints?"

"Miss Ramirez, let me tell you something. I've seen every sort of madness and stupidity in the criminal element. I've worked cases where we've found the perpetrator with the victim at his feet and

128

the weapon in his hand and a hundred witnesses who saw him do it, and he'll swear to God, the Blessed Virgin Mary and all the saints in Heaven that he's been set up." He sighed with exasperation, as if trying to explain nuclear physics to a kindergartner.

"Has the boyfriend been checked out as a suspect?" Lacking sufficient proof, I didn't mention my suspicions about Bradley's involvement with drugs. I had other plans for how to use that information.

"Yes, Miss Ramirez," he said condescendingly. "He was checked out thoroughly. I know better than you do that most homicide victims are killed by people they know. Believe me, we haven't overlooked that possibility. He's clean as a whistle."

"Any progress on IDing the victim?"

"No comment."

"Any luck on finding out the identity of the anonymous tipster who called in the location of Toni's body?"

"No comment. Look, I'm not going to stay on the phone with you all day justifying every move we've made in this investigation," Gibbs said firmly. "I have police work to do."

"Thanks for your time, detective," I said calmly and courteously. "I'll be in touch."

Damn, if only I had Terry's connections and inside information. I entertained a brief fantasy of being able to extract details from Gibbs by threatening to revealing some embarrassing secret — that he wore a toupee, cheated on his wife, or had been in rehab.

What was my next move? It was too soon to call Faith Brooks. It was time to see Toni's brother.

* * * * *

Though sullen and uncommunicative on the phone, Paul Stewart agreed to meet me at the Student Union cafeteria on Thursday.

The decor had remained the same — modern hideous. Avocado green, pumpkin orange, and bronze vinyl chairs and benches, faux wood grain table tops, and black-, brown-, and gold-flecked tiles made for an aesthetic horror, but I felt at home here.

I was drinking my second cup of acrid coffee when he came up to my table, a corner booth I had often used for studying between classes when I was a student.

"Paul, you've grown up so much," I said.

Saying nothing, he sat across from me. The family resemblance was strong — he had Toni's curly brown hair, nose, jaw line, and deep brown eyes. But on him, the result suggested peevishness rather than self-possession. He was wearing a sweat suit with his fraternity letters on the pants and shirt.

"Paul, I'm so sorry about your sister."

"Yeah, well, thanks," he said, looking down at the table.

"I know this must be very hard for you, but I'm going to ask you some questions. You and Toni were very close, and it's possible she may have confided something to you that may help me track down her killer."

"What makes you so sure that this Leonard guy didn't do it?" he said. "They found the murder weapon on him and everything. Doesn't that close the case?"

"I think it's worth looking into. Anyway, I'm

130

stubborn," I said. "Was your sister open with you about what happened in San Francisco?"

He twirled the drawstring on the hood of his sweat shirt. "What do you mean?"

"Did she tell you about her relationship with Faith Brooks?"

"They worked together." He kept looking down.

"They were also lovers, Paul. Did she talk about that?"

His face turned crimson. "My sister was not a dyke," he hissed. He stood up to leave.

"Paul, please. Toni was closer to you than anybody else. You may be the only one who could help point me in the right direction."

"I've told the police all I know." He shifted from one foot to the other, his hands shoved deep in his pockets.

"Sit down. We won't discuss that anymore." I could see it made him uncomfortable. Maybe he just wasn't mature enough to accept the idea of a lesbian sister.

He sat, his face still ruddy from my question.

Just then, two young men stopped by our table. One was a squatty blond who looked like he spent a lot of time in the weight room. The other was a tall, thin boy with a black crewcut.

"What's up, little bro?" the squatty one said to Paul.

"Nothing, Dweezer," Paul said. "Just talking to a friend."

"Hi, I'm Carmen Ramirez. I was a friend of Paul's sister, Toni Stewart," I said to the pair. I didn't expect Paul to have the manners to introduce me.

The tall boy stood silently as Dweezer asked, "So, did you go to school here?"

"I did. This spring, it'll be five years since I graduated. I can't believe it," I replied.

"What sorority?" he said. "You know, I've dated girls from nearly all the houses on Sorority Row."

"I wasn't in a sorority," I said.

Dweezer eyed me suspiciously. "No luck during Rush Week?" he said in an accent straight out of Chicago.

Rush Week was a ridiculous orgy of snobbery held every August the week before classes opened at FCU. Incoming freshmen tried desperately to persuade the school's seven sororities and seven fraternities to accept them for membership. For women, that meant huge expenditures for wardrobe and hairstyles and a non-stop week of dinners, teas and parties — all designed to weed out "undesirables." On the men's side, students were scrutinized based on what kind of car their daddies and mommies bought them, how many Ralph Lauren Polo shirts they brought along, how much beer they could swill down at a string of keg parties and how well they fit in with the other "dudes."

Despite all that the fraternities and sororities said to the contrary, selections were based on class, race, ethnicity, social polish and physical appearance. Special consideration was given to legacies, sons or daughters of previous members. Fraternities and sororities were for wealthy or upper-middle-class heterosexual white kids with solid Northern European roots and trim waistlines. Black, Jewish, Native American, working-class, visibly queer or overweight students need not apply.

On the last night of Rush Week, students were sealed in their rooms. The lucky ones received one or more envelopes with their names on it. Inside was an invitation to join. Once students made the first cut of receiving bids, they faced an apprenticeship as pledges, during which they were required to prove their loyalty and worthiness. Full members demanded absolute obedience from their pledges, who were required to run errands, do laundry, and fetch snacks for their future brothers or sisters. Many of the men were hazed — spanked, verbally abused, and forced to drink potentially dangerous amounts of alcohol. The women preferred more subtle social pressure, putting their prospective members through a series of formal and informal parties, teas, and dinners — all designed to ensure that their girls were made of the right stuff.

After this second period of scrutiny, each frat and sorority took a vote on whether to accept its pledges for the final cut — initiation. A single negative vote meant the would-be member was blackballed, forced to join the ranks of FCU's unaffiliated students, otherwise known as the common herd. Those who made the cut won the privilege of wearing Greek letters on their clothing, attending countless theme parties for their own kind, competing in numerous athletic competitions, preparing tissue-paper floats for homecoming week and forcing future freshmen to grovel for the right to belong to their group.

After seventeen years of rigid conformity in the Baptist Church, I had no interest in jumping through hoops in order to belong to any group. "I didn't attend Rush Week," I said to Dweezer.

"That's a shame. I knew the Deltas took a

Hispanic —" He stopped when I shot him a warning glance.

"How nice of them," I said.

He seemed embarrassed. "It's always nice to see old alums on campus," he said. "Little bro, you got a minute?"

"Sure, Dweez," Paul replied.

The three of them walked outside to the cafeteria courtyard. Through floor-to-ceiling windows, I could see the exchange between them. Speaking heatedly, Dweezer pointed his finger at Paul. Paul's back was to me, but his posture suggested submissiveness.

Paul returned, his face just as flushed as when he left.

"Everything okay?" I said. "He seemed pretty angry at you."

He nodded. "Dweezer, his real name is Donald, is the pledge master at my frat. I'm on the initiation committee this year and I missed a couple of meetings."

"Pledge master? Is that like a drill sergeant?" I said, barely suppressing a sneer.

"He's in charge of the pledges. He's pretty much God at Sigma Alpha Sigma."

What a distinction, I thought, but I decided not to burden Paul with my opinion. I wanted to keep him as friendly and talkative as possible. "The police found another body out where Toni was found," I said. "White guy, five-seven, early twenties, black hair. Does that sound like anyone Toni may have been hanging out with or dating?"

"Toni wouldn't have dated a wimp like that."

The answer struck me as bizarre. "What makes you think he was a wimp?"

"You said he was five-seven, didn't you? She didn't go for short guys. Bradley's well over six feet." He pulled a napkin out of the holder and shredded it.

He was so nervous. "Did Bradley and Toni ever have troubles?"

"She complained about him once in a while. Nothing major." He stacked the salt shaker on the napkin holder.

"Did she ever talk about breaking up with him?"

"She talked about it all the time, but I don't think she was ever serious about it." He added the pepper shaker to the top of the salt.

"Was she serious about marrying him?"

"As serious as she ever got about anything." He shredded another napkin.

"Did you ever see Bradley get angry with her, maybe lose his temper or threaten her?"

"She was the one who always got mad. He took whatever she handed out."

"Did Bradley every hit her or abuse her?"

"I'd buy tickets to that," he said with a caustic laugh, adding fiercely, "Toni didn't take shit off anyone, least of all Brad. Nobody could kick her ass." Tears filled his eyes.

I patted his arm. "I'm so sorry. We all miss her very much."

He pulled away.

"Did Toni ever suggest that Bradley was ever involved in any illegal activity?"

"What do you mean?"

"Drugs."

His eyes shifted. "No. Never. Look, I've got to go. I have a class in half an hour."

I watched him walk away.

Paul was right. Toni had to be the dominant partner in any relationship. She had been with me, and I'm sure it was the same story with Bradley. But suppose he had quietly resented her for years, his rage finally exploding into murder when he found out about her relationship with Faith. He had been polite with me for years, and then suddenly turned on me. Maybe he'd done the same thing with Toni, on a much bigger scale.

Or maybe Toni had found out that Bradley was selling drugs and demanded he stop because she was worried it would destroy his chances for a law career.

And the other body? Had Bradley killed two people? Maybe Toni was seeing this guy on the side and he killed them both. She was so damned secretive, anything was possible.

Friday, the police released the identity of the second victim found at Sequoyah. Desmond Allen was a twenty-one-year-old hairdresser living in a studio apartment in the university district. Before his disappearance, he had worked at the trendy Headquarters salon in the city's newly fashionable Fifteenth Street district.

The night Allen's ID was released, the *Times* and every other news organization in town ran his photo. After a long shift, I headed home.

Charles was reading on the sofa when I got in.

"Look at this," I said, handing him the front page. "They finally ID'd the guy who was found at Lake Sequoyah."

Charles stared at the newspaper in disbelief. "Hey, I know this guy. I ran into him half a dozen times at Wilde's."

"No kidding. So he was gay?"

"Definitely," Charles said. "He even gave me his card."

After digging through his wallet, Charles handed the business card to me. It was black with silver lettering: HEADQUARTERS, A FULL-SERVICE SALON FOR A MORE BEAUTIFUL YOU. DESMOND ALLEN, HAIR STYLIST.

"He said he'd give me a free shampoo and manicure if I ever came by," Charles said.

"I wonder if Toni knew him. And I wonder if it's just a coincidence that both she and Desmond were gay." I looked at the black card, wishing it could answer me.

Saturday, I dropped by Headquarters, a shiny chrome and mirrored salon with throbbing disco music.

The receptionist, a pleasant young woman with brilliant maroon hair and matching lipstick, didn't recognize Toni when I showed her the snapshot I'd brought along.

"I don't think she's ever been in here, and honestly, I'm pretty good with faces."

"Did she ever call here for Desmond?"

"I've been here five days a weeks for the past year, and I don't recall taking a call from her. Most of the personal calls for Desmond were from men. You know, the police have already asked me all this."

"Can you check your appointment book and see if she was ever a customer?" I said. "It's really important."

"That would take so long, and I don't have the time. These phones ring all day long," she said, pointing to the desk to emphasize her workload. "If you want to come back around seven, that's when we close. I hang around to clean up. You could go through it then if you like."

That wouldn't do. I had to work that evening. "How about if I send by my friends to go through the book?"

"Sure. They just have to be out by eight, because that's when I lock up and leave."

Charles and Julia were less than thrilled when I asked them to go to the salon to read through the salon's appointment book for the last eight months, but they agreed to do it.

I called Julia on my break.

"Only one Tony was on the books," she told me, "and that was a man. He comes in every week for a beard trim and every six weeks for a haircut and shampoo."

"Damn," I said. "I can't figure out the connection between the two of them."

"I don't know either, but Charles told me to tell you that he's made an appointment for a bikini waxing next week."

I heard his maniacal laughter in the background. "Very funny. Well thanks for checking, kids."

Faith Brooks got right to the point when I called her Sunday afternoon. It had been nearly a week since I gave her the bad news about Toni. "Who gave you this number?"

"Directory assistance," I said. "I'm really sorry about the way I broke the news to you."

She didn't respond.

"Let me tell you a little more about why I called. I'm a journalist, and I'm looking into Toni's murder. She was a friend of mine, hence my interest in the case."

She said nothing.

"Did Toni make any enemies while she was in San Francisco?"

"No. I don't think so. None that I observed, anyway, and I was very close to her — between working and living together."

"Did Toni ever mention having any trouble with her boyfriend? Was he ever abusive? Was he involved in any criminal activity?"

"Boyfriend?" she said in disbelief.

"Bradley Pennington."

"She never mentioned having a boyfriend, and she never mentioned knowing anybody by that name."

"She had dated him since high school. They were engaged. The wedding was set for this summer."

"You're telling me Toni was straight?" She clearly stunned.

"She could have been bisexual, a curious straight,

139

or a lesbian having trouble coming to terms with her sexuality. I can't say for sure."

"And what was your relationship with her?" Her tone was bitter.

"We were best friends for three years. I was also in love with her. She was dating Bradley that whole time. I was afraid to act on my lesbianism, so it was very convenient to fall in love with my best friend. We split up on bad terms, back in eighty-three. I didn't see her again until the fall, when she joined a lesbian and gay group my lover is involved in."

"I see." Her voice was steely.

"Did Toni ever mention knowing a guy named Desmond Allen?"

"Another ex-lover, I presume," she said wearily.

"He's a gay man whose body was found near where Toni's was. I'm trying to see if the two of them were somehow connected."

"She never said anything about him to me, but apparently that wasn't unusual for Toni," she said caustically.

"I know how much you must be hurting right now," I said.

She was silent for a while. Then she started crying. "I loved her. I really did. I found out that she was messing around, and I just couldn't accept that. She said she was sorry, that she wanted to give it another try. But I couldn't. I thought we needed time apart. I didn't want to be with someone I couldn't count on. Now to hear that everything between us was false . . ." Her voice trailed off.

"Toni held everyone at bay," I said. "But she could be wonderful, charming, charismatic. You have to treasure what was good between you and let the rest go."

She said nothing.

"Please let me know if you can think of anything else that could help us figure out who did it."

The phone went dead.

The following Saturday night, after I got off work, Charles, Julia, and I went to Wilde's to ask some questions.

The night before, when I finished my shift, I had laid the groundwork for our trip with a visit to my old buddy Crystal Reeves, owner of Crystal's Tavern. I arrived about a half-hour before closing time. The decor was tacky — Christmas lights twinkled in the bar year-round and black velvet paintings of nude blondes with enormous breasts adorned the walls. Next to the dance floor was a huge plaque reading: STAY HEALTHY, EAT YOUR HONEY. And in preparation for Valentine's Day, the place was decked out in red hearts and Cupids.

Crystal — a tough-as-nails West Texan with a snow-white crewcut and a wide, impressive physique — readily agreed to let the owners of Wilde's know that we were coming and to vouch for our good character.

"By the way," she told me as she poured a seltzer and lime for me, "you trying out again for the team? They're bowling Sunday afternoons. Debby's got a bad back. We could use you as an alternate, you know, just in case she locks up stiff as a board."

141

"I'll think about it."

She lit a filterless Camel and winked at me. "If you run into any trouble with this killing you're looking into, you know who to call. I love a good brawl."

By midnight, when we arrived at Wilde's, the place was packed. It was impossible to question anybody over the loud music, so we waited outside, by the door, to question patrons on their way in or out.

Quite a few people remembered Desmond. Some recalled Toni's dispute with Leonard. Nobody remembered seeing Desmond and Toni together. And no one had seen Bradley.

Later, when business thinned out as closing time approached, Charles and Julia questioned the cocktail waiters while I talked with the bartender, a tall, blond, heavily muscled man with a brush cut and handlebar mustache. He was wearing skin-tight jeans and, despite the freezing weather outside, a tank top. Wilde's was new and modern, the bar easily three times bigger than Crystal's.

"Hi there. I was wondering if I could ask you a couple of questions." I placed pictures of Toni, Desmond, Leonard, and Bradley on the bar. "Did you ever see these people here at the bar?"

He studied the photos.

"Desmond and Toni were found dead near Lake Sequoyah. They're both gay, and my friend over there, the tall guy by the jukebox, says he remembers seeing Desmond here. Toni was also here, involved in a fight with this guy," I said, pointing to the photo of Leonard, "the one who's about to stand trial for her murder."

"What's your interest in all this?"

"I'm a journalist and a friend of Crystal's."

"Crystal Reeves?" he said. "That woman literally saved my life."

"She did?"

He slapped the bar and smiled broadly. "When I first came to town about ten years ago, I was only eighteen, scrawny as hell. This was before I lifted weights and learned how to take care of myself, mind you. Anyway, I had just gotten off a Greyhound bus from Lake Charles, Louisiana, and these two soldiers spotted me as gay and started making trouble. They dragged me off into the alley behind the depot to do God-only-knows-what. Crystal, who was there to drop off her girlfriend, punched both of them out, and then we took off in her pickup truck. She let me stay at her place for two weeks until I could get on my feet. How is she?"

"Feisty as ever," I said. If somebody told me that Crystal had scaled Mount Everest or walked barefoot across the Mojave Desert, I wouldn't have been surprised. Crystal was as tough as they come. "Anyway," I told the bartender, "I'm looking into the Stewart case. I think there may be a connection between her death and Desmond's. Leonard Martin says he's been framed, and I'm checking out his story."

He continued to look at the photos. "I've seen three of them. I threw Leonard out myself that night when he was bugging this woman — told him not to come back for a month. Des was here all the time, and Toni was too, although I never saw them together. Of course, this place gets busy, so I couldn't possibly see everything that goes on."

"Did you ever see Desmond with Leonard?"

"No. I don't think so."

"How about this guy?" I pointed to the photo of Bradley, which I had photocopied out of the FCU yearbook.

"I've never seen him."

I handed him my card. "Thanks for your time. If you think of anything else, please call me."

He waved at me as I left. "Be sure to tell Crystal that Phil said hello."

Later, at an all-night pancake house, we compared notes. The waiters told Charles and Julia that they remembered Toni, Leonard and Desmond, but nobody saw Toni and Desmond together, or Desmond with Leonard. And everyone drew a blank on Bradley's photo.

"I just remembered something," I said. "The night Toni called me, right before she disappeared, there was loud music in the background. She could have been at Wilde's. She told me she would give me a news tip if I agreed to protect somebody. Then she clammed up because somebody left."

"Well," Julia said, "we've got to find somebody who knows why she was there that night."

"But who?" I said. "Toni was extremely secretive, and when she wasn't that, she was downright dishonest."

Monday morning, another round of phone calls

proved fruitless. I spoke with Toni's mother, who didn't know anything about her daughter's trip to the bar. Bradley wouldn't return my calls. And based on the way he had acted last time, I thought it unwise to speak with him face to face. My last hope was Paul, who was also avoiding me.

Monday afternoon, a boy with a white Polo shirt, Levis and penny loafers met me at the door of the Sigma Alpha Sigma house, a three-story, red-brick colonial on FCU's Fraternity Row.

Frat row wasn't exactly familiar to me. During my student days, I heard plenty of stories about what went on along frat row on weekend nights — usually wild parties designed to foster quick, easy, alcohol-fueled sexual encounters between the frat members and their women guests. Since boys weren't my cup of tea, I gave their party scene wide berth.

"I'm Carmen Ramirez. I'm here to see Paul Stewart," I said.

"Come on in," said the boy at the door, eying me warily. "His room is Three B, on the third floor."

I walked through the spacious common room, which was deserted, except for two men playing pool. The room had a huge fireplace with roaring fire, its mantel decorated by a coat of arms — a two-foot-high blue, red and gold shield with the frat's Greek letters, a sun, moon, and two crossed swords, and a Greek motto across the bottom. Several large plaid sofas and armchairs were arranged in front of a big-screen television, which was tuned to MTV. The men looked up from their billiards as I passed. I heard them mutter something, probably directed at me. I was almost certain I heard one of them say "piece of ass." My face got hot, but I pretended I hadn't heard them.

An elderly Hispanic man polished the parquet floor in the dining room with an electric buffer.

"May I just walk up?" I asked the boy who had let me in.

He shrugged. "Whatever."

As I headed for the stairs, I heard more muttering from the pool players and the kid who had let me in. I was grateful not to meet anyone else on the stairway.

Paul, clad in yet another Sigma Alpha Sigma sweat suit, was less than cordial when I knocked on his door. "What the hell are you doing here?" he said angrily.

"I need to talk to you," I said, "and you won't return my calls." It had been a week and a half since I had last seen him.

Paul looked into the hall, as if he expected someone else to be with me. "Okay. Come in." He probably didn't want anyone to think I was his girlfriend.

His room was small and darkly paneled, furnished with two twin beds, two desks, bookshelves and a wardrobe. A dart board and numerous *Playboy* and *Penthouse* centerfold shots decorated the wall. I pulled a chair out from the desk and sat there while Paul perched uneasily on the bed.

"I don't have much time," he said.

"Are you expecting your roommate? We can talk somewhere else if you'd be more comfortable."

He said nothing.

"It's okay. I'll be brief," I said, showing him a photo of Desmond. "You're sure you never saw Toni with this guy?"

"I saw this picture on the news, and the cops have already asked me about him." His agitation was growing.

"Okay, okay," I said, trying to settle him down. "I have one more question, and it's very important that you answer honestly. It may be the only way we can catch your sister's killer."

He looked out the window.

"I'm convinced that these killings are connected. The only link I have been able to find is the bar Wilde's. Ever hear of it?"

"Everybody knows that's a queer bar," he said, looking back at me angrily.

"Your sister went there more than once. So did Desmond. The night before she disappeared, Toni called me from a place with loud music in the background. I think she may have been at the bar. She hinted that she had a news tip for me, but I had to agree to protect somebody involved. Do you know why she was there? Did she ever tell you anything about it? Was she in some sort of trouble?"

"My sister was not a queer, and she never went to queer bars. Period!" he said. His face turned a brilliant red. "Look, I've got a French exam. I've got to study. Plus I've got to help decorate the house for the big Valentine's dance. Can you please just go?"

I looked at him. "Would you mind walking me out? I was a little uncomfortable on the way in."

"I've got to hit the books," he said, shrugging at me. "Nobody's going to bother you."

As I walked through the living room, I confronted

more staring and muttering from the two pool players and the boy who let me in. They were all dressed alike — in Levis, button-down shirts and penny loafers — and wore the same short haircuts. I looked around for the cleaning man, but he was gone.

Why the hell were they acting this way? Because I was an outsider? A woman? A Latina? Because my short hair and jeans identified me as a dyke?

With smug faces, they laughed and poked one another in the ribs.

When I reached the door, they broke into a chorus of unintelligible hoots and catcalls.

I slammed the door and walked briskly to my car.

That afternoon, back at my apartment, I finally got through to Bradley Pennington.

"What do you mean by leaving a threatening message on my answering machine, Bradley?"

He was immediately hostile. "I thought I told you to leave me alone."

"So you admit it," I said.

"I don't have to talk to you."

"Not so fast, pal. I'd like to know what you and your pot-smoking roommate were up to the other day," I demanded.

"What the hell are you talking about?" he said angrily.

"You know very well that I followed you to Murray Park and I saw the both of you make a drug buy. Are you pushing the stuff too?"

"You're being ridiculous," he said, his voice tight.

"The police might not think so. If I call them,

you have to either get rid of your stash, which would be very expensive, or go to jail, which would be very unpleasant. And I don't think the law school administration and the Bar Association would take a drug conviction so lightly."

"You fucking dyke."

I was getting awfully sick of the "D" word. "Call me a dyke one more time, Bradley, and I'll call the cops on you right this second, I swear to God."

"Okay, okay. I get the message," he said sullenly.

"Did Toni find out about your drug dealing? Is that why you had to kill her?"

Bradley paused. "Damn you, Carmen. I would never hurt her. Yes, I sell pot with Jackson — a few bags here and there when I need the money."

"Why would you need money with your background?" Like Toni, he was also wealthy.

He sighed. "My old man lost a lot of money when the bottom dropped out of oil prices. He's cut back on my allowance."

His answer infuriated me. "Have you ever thought of working for a living? You know, getting a job?"

"Spare me the sermon," he said wearily. "I really don't care whether you approve of my work ethic."

I put aside my anger. "So Toni found out about your activities?"

There was a long silence. "I didn't hide it from her. She thought I was stupid to sell with Jackson. He's so heavily into pot that she thought he would make a mistake and get us both thrown in jail."

"So she threatened to turn you in?"

"No, of course not. You know as well as I do that she used to smoke pot back as an undergrad."

He was right. I couldn't imagine Toni turning

anybody in for involvement with marijuana — even selling. "Then why all the hostility the other day? You and Stewart both were treating me like Public Enemy Number One."

"All right, all right," he said peevishly. "When Toni came back from the West Coast, she was depressed. Mr. Stewart went through her stuff, looking for anything suspicious — pot, pills. He found a diary. Your name was mentioned. Toni was hung up on you."

My heart nearly stopped.

"He point-blank asked her what was going on. She said she had been in love with Faith and they had broken up. But he blamed you for putting her on that path." Bradley paused. "Then, he told me. I wasn't shocked. There were lots of signs. She was such a tomboy, she was so close to you. I saw the way she looked at women when she didn't think I was watching her. Plus, she never was all that attracted to me. I knew. I just couldn't admit it to myself."

"So what happened?" I said, reeling from all this information.

He took a deep breath. "Mr. Stewart asked me to start seeing her again, to 'straighten her out,' so to speak. I'd never gotten over Toni, so I was happy to go along. But she wasn't interested in me anymore, in a sexual way, and she was honest about it. After her relationship with Faith, there was no question in her mind. She knew she was a lesbian. But she was depressed over losing you and then Faith. She was trapped and didn't know what to do with her life. Her father offered her law school, if she cleaned up her act."

"My God," I said, "poor Toni."

"I'm not the ogre you think I am," Bradley said sadly. "I still loved her. I really did. I never pressured her to do anything. We started going out again, just for her parents' benefit. We told them we were engaged. Her old man stayed off her back. He was happy to believe she'd been straight all along, that you and San Francisco were responsible for her strange behavior. Toni got to live in comfort with law school fully financed by her parents. I just wanted her to be happy."

Happy and comfortable living a lie, I thought.

"You're not going to turn me in, are you?"

I thought about it. I didn't approve of his activities, but I couldn't bring myself to turn him over to the cops. "I won't report you, but if you have any sense at all, you'll get out of the drug business before you wind up dead or in prison. It was easy enough for me to spot, and I'm an amateur. One call from a nosy neighbor could destroy your career."

I hung up, deeply depressed. I had hit a dead end. There was absolutely no evidence that Bradley had killed Toni. And I didn't get the feeling he was lying to me.

But if he didn't kill her, who did?

The following Saturday night, my phone rang fifteen minutes away from first edition deadline.

"Carmen, something weird's going on," Charles said. Loud dance music pumped in the background. "Meet me and Julia at Wilde's. How soon do you think you can be here?"

I didn't dare ask Newman, who was already glowering at me, when the shift would end. But because Sunday's paper was the largest of the week, deadlines were earlier. "Not for a few hours. Probably eleven-thirty."

"Carmen," Newman said, "would you mind setting aside your love life to help your colleagues put the newspaper out?"

"I gotta go. I'm on deadline."

"We'll wait for you in the parking lot," Charles said.

Ten seconds later, a message from Newman appeared on my screen: "Make yourself available for a meeting at the end of the shift."

At eleven-fifteen, Newman, sweaty and nervous, sat across from me in the news conference room. "I can't have my operation come to a halt because of your love life."

"Jerry, in the first place, your comment about my love life is completely out of line. In the second place, I was on the phone less than thirty seconds."

"And for thirty seconds, all your colleagues were distracted and unable to perform their tasks," he said.

"The newsroom is a noisy place, the phones ring all night, and anyone who can't handle that shouldn't be in this business," I said. I was less than pleasant, but Newman hated my guts, and there was not much I could do to make the situation worse.

His face reddened. "I don't like your attitude."

"I'm aware of that," I said. "Short of groveling at

your feet and kissing your ass, there's not much I could do to please you."

"I write your performance reviews," his voice high and shrill. "I could do a lot of damage to your file."

"Give it your best shot, Jerry. And don't leave one detail out," I said, storming out of the conference room.

CHAPTER EIGHT

At eleven forty-five, the parking lot outside Wilde's was full, so I parked a block and a half away. The weather was frigid and when the wind gusted out of the north, it was unbearable. I was still walking in darkness when I felt a hand on my shoulder.

I wheeled around. There stood Charles, with Julia behind him.

"You scared me," I said, my heart racing.

"Sorry. I saw you drive past, and I didn't want you to blow our cover," Charles said.

"Cover?" I said.

"This was stuffed in the door when Julia and I came back from the movies," he said, handing me a typed note.

IF YOU WANT TO KNOW WHO KILLED TONI STEWART AND DESMOND ALLEN, SHOW UP AT WILDE'S TONIGHT.

"Check out that boy standing there in the plaid coat by the door to the club," he said.

A boy in a red-and-black plaid Mackinaw coat approached a man leaving the bar, briefly spoke to him, and then the man walked away.

"So?" I said.

"He's cruising," he said.

"In this weather? Why not go into the club?" I said.

"I got a good look at him. He's probably only eighteen or nineteen, and the bar is really strict about IDs," he said. "Julia and I walked into the bar. He stopped me at the door and asked me if I wanted to go party with him at Lake Sequoyah."

"So there's our connection," Julia said. "Desmond, Toni, Wilde's and Lake Sequoyah."

An icy wind lashed us. Despite a sweater, parka, wool socks and gloves, I was cut to the bone. "Damn, it's cold," I said.

Charles said, "Oh, honey, I was up in Minnesota once in February —"

"I really don't want to hear it," I said. "This right now is the coldest it can possibly be anywhere in the universe. Okay? Just humor me."

"You're the boss," Charles said. "We've been

watching him for well over an hour. He's been approaching every man who walks by."

"It gets weirder," Julia said. "See that black van over there?"

A new, black Chevrolet Astro van with out-of-county Oklahoma plates was parked just across the street from the bar.

"Every fifteen minutes or so, the guy in plaid walks over and talks to the driver," Charles said. "This must be what the note is all about."

"We've got to call the cops," I said.

"And tell them what?" Charles said. "As soon as a cop car shows up, if they even come, the van takes off and the guy by the door says, 'I was just asking people for a cigarette.' "

"What's the alternative?" I asked.

"We wait until he picks somebody up. Then we tail them."

"It's way too dangerous," I said.

"I agree," Julia added. "Whoever sent that note might be trying to flush us out, lure us into a remote area and kill us. If this guy and the goons in the van are the guilty parties, they've already killed twice and they won't hesitate to do it again. Besides, if we don't have proof to take to the police, we're no better off than we were before."

"It's not necessarily a trap," I said. "It could well be that the person who wrote the note knows who killed Toni but is afraid of exposure. Don't forget, an anonymous tipster phoned in the location of Toni's body. But Julia is right. We do need evidence. Charles, what about your video camera?"

"That's it!" he said.

We devised a plan. Julia returned to the apartment for the camera while Charles and I kept an eye on the guy in the plaid coat.

She returned, armed with the camera, extra sweaters and wool caps, two sets of thermal underwear, and a thermos of hot coffee. After Charles and I ducked into the restrooms of a Speedy Petey con- venience store across the street to change into our extra layers, we went over our strategy.

"We watch the guy until he picks somebody up," I said. "Charles and I will follow them. Julia, you drive home in Charles's car and wait to hear from us. If we don't get back by a set time, you call the cops."

"I hate it," Julia said.

"We know what they're going to try. As long as they don't discover us, we're fine," Charles said.

For more than an hour, we watched the guy in plaid chat up patrons leaving and entering the bar.

I looked at my watch. Nearly two a.m.

"It's almost closing time," I said. "I'm afraid we're going to strike out."

"No, no," Charles said. "This is the witching hour. Even Godzilla could get picked up right now."

Just then, a man in a tan overcoat approached Plaid Man. After a brief chat, they got into a late-model red Mustang with tinted windows and Missouri plates.

"Okay, Julia," I said. "It's two a.m. If we haven't gotten in touch with you by three-thirty, call the cops."

I embraced Julia.

"I love you both," she said.

"Me too," I said.

She quickly hugged Charles. "Watch out, both of you."

Charles and I ran to my Civic a block and a half away and returned to the bar just as the Mustang turned right onto Eleventh, a busy four-lane street. We followed.

"We're not alone. The van is right behind us," Charles said.

I switched to the right lane to let the Astro get ahead. Just then, I noticed a rental agency sticker on the back of the van.

Tailing them east, we crossed two major avenues before the Mustang and van turned north on Sherman. A mile north, we crossed General Boulevard into the north side of town. They were headed to the park, all right.

We had them in our sight until the traffic light at Oak. They made the light and we didn't.

"What do we do now?" Charles said.

"Keep heading toward the park," I said.

"What if they take him someplace else?"

"I can't think about that."

"We can't stop here," I said to Charles as we spotted the car and van in a dirt lot near Lake

Sequoyah. "They'll know we're following." We drove a mile or so up the road to another parking area.

I knew the area well from my Girl Scout days, when I used to spend hours around the lake on nature walks with my troop. "There's a trail that goes all the way around the lake. The path back here through these trees meets up with the lake path," I said as I parked the car. "It's shorter than the main road. I've got flashlights and some binoculars in the car. Should we bring them along?"

"Sure," Charles said, "but once we get close, we should avoid the flashlights, except for emergencies."

"How close do we have to get for that camera to work in the dark?" I said.

"If it's pitch dark," he said, "it won't do us any good, no matter how close we are. Without a light source, it's worthless. We just have to hope for the best." He put the camera in his backpack and slung it over his shoulder.

We hiked quickly, without talking. My eyes adjusted to the darkness, and soon, I was able to stop running into branches and pick my way through the woods. After about half an hour, Charles held a finger to his mouth, then pointed across from us. In the distance, I could make out lights moving through the trees. It must have been the men from the parking lot. I nodded, and we continued, more aware of our need to be quiet.

As we drew closer, we could hear the men tramping through the woods. Charles pointed to a bush and indicated we should stop there. We waited and watched in silence. Charles perched the video camera on his shoulder and pointed it toward the source of noise. I pulled out my binoculars, but I couldn't see anything. If only I had some of those cool night-vision glasses you see in the movies. Just then, a flash of light. Our hikers were helping our cause by lighting a fire. From the looks of it, they were going heavy on the lighter fluid. The fire grew brighter. I estimated that roughly thirty men — all wearing ski masks or scarves over their faces — had gathered there. Smaller points of light appeared as they passed candles among one another.

Behold the hour is here.

Was that chanting?

As this initiate seeks to join our brotherhood . . .

A blindfolded man was pushed into the center of the crowd.

"Behold our disciple," said a man in an orange hunter's parka and a ski mask. Despite the stilted, theatrical delivery, the voice sounded familiar.

"Master, I am not worthy to be counted among you," said the blindfolded figure, the young man in the red and black plaid Mackinaw coat we had seen at Wilde's.

"You must pass the test," the familiar voice intoned.

Where had I heard him before? His accent made it apparent that he wasn't from Oklahoma.

"First, you must swear to keep the secrets of the sacred and mysterious rites of our brotherhood, even if threatened with torture or death," the man in orange said.

"I swear," said the blindfolded man.

"Are you ready?"

160

"I accept the sacred duties of our illustrious brotherhood. I am ready, Master."

The boy dropped his trousers. The Master opened his coat and pulled out a paddle.

We watched as each man in the crowd took a swing at Plaid Man's bare butt.

"Oh Lord," I whispered to Charles. "It's some kind of initiation."

"I may be able to sell this video for big bucks," he replied.

The chanting resumed. *The final test awaits. The final test awaits.*

"Make him suffer," the Master ordered. "This is my command."

Blindfolded, bound and gagged, the man in the tan overcoat from the bar was thrown at the feet of the initiate.

Tentatively, the initiate, no longer blindfolded, kicked the man in the stomach.

"Jesus," I said, feeling the blow with him.

"Harder," the group commanded.

The boy kicked again, this time harder.

"Harder! Harder! Harder!" the mob cried out.

And then, the Master shouted above all the others: "Destroy the faggot!"

We watched as the other boys took turns kicking and punching the victim, who was writhing to ward off the blows.

We had to do something. But what? We were miles from a phone, we were outnumbered, and we had no weapons. And it was plain that they would kill us, just as they had Toni, if we intervened.

The violent gang continued to work over the man, who was no longer writhing. He must have passed out. He couldn't withstand this savagery much longer.

"Charles, I'm afraid they're going to kill him. I have a plan," I said, "but we have to move now."

"Why don't we just sneak out and call the cops?" Charles said.

"He may be dead by then," I said.

Nodding in agreement, Charles returned the camera to his backpack. "You carry this," he said. "I may have to fight them, and it will give us a better chance if both my arms are free."

Silently, we moved closer to the scene of the crime. When we were about fifteen yards away and still covered by the underbrush, we made our move. I shined both flashlights toward the group, and Charles cupped his hands around his mouth. He barked out, "This is the police. This gathering is unlawful. Disperse immediately."

The boys, with blood on their hands and sweat on their frenzied faces, looked toward us. I hoped the flashlights I was shining toward them would keep them from seeing we weren't cops.

"I repeat: This is the police," Charles shouted.

The boys looked around at one another. Chaos was about to break out. The Master turned around and looked toward us.

And then, I caught his eyes through the holes of his ski mask. It was Dweezer, Paul Stewart's fraternity brother.

For a moment that seemed like an eternity, nobody did anything.

And then, Dweezer called to his gang: "Those aren't cops. Get them."

"Carmen, run," Charles said. "Get help. I'll try to hold them off."

Terrified and unable to move, I looked at him.

"Go now!" he said. I saw him pick up a large branch. Then I took off running. I knew I had to get help if either of us was going to get out of this alive.

As shouts and screams arose behind me, I ran as hard as my legs, rubbery with fear, could carry me.

My stomach heaving, my lungs ablaze, I ran and ran, sheer terror propelling me. I could hear nothing but my heart beating wildly and blood rushing in my ears. Branches tore at my face, but I felt nothing.

At last, the car was in sight.

I pulled out my keys and made a run for the door.

Suddenly, I felt a sharp blow, more stunning than painful, on the side of my head.

"Hey, little rabbit," said the man. I recognized him immediately. He was the tall, thin fellow with the black crewcut who had been with Dweezer that day in the cafeteria. He had three other frat members with him. "You're coming with us."

Just before they grabbed me, I let the backpack slip off my shoulder.

The four frat boys led me back to the parking lot where the van and red Mustang were parked. Three other cars were there in the lot, probably belonging to the rest of the gang.

Dweezer, standing in the middle of his henchmen, recognized me at once.

"So, little bro," he said, "what have you been telling your friend Carmen?"

Paul Stewart emerged behind the van. "Nothing, Dweez. I swear to Christ."

"He's telling the truth," I said.

"Who asked you?" Dweezer said.

"What did you do with the other two?" I demanded.

"You'll find out soon enough," he said.

My heart lurched with fear.

"Put her in the van," he ordered.

The four boys who had captured me at the car dragged me to the van and pinned me against the door. Two forced my arms together and one held my feet while the one who had called me "little rabbit" bound my wrists with duct tape.

My mind raced as the man squatted to bind my ankles. "Tell Dweezer that a friend of ours is going to call the police if we're not back safe and sound very soon," I said to the man with the duct tape. "You can't get away with this. Cut your losses now and let us go. They know where we are. Your rental van can be traced."

The foursome threw me into the van. I struck the floor hard, the rough carpet scraping my face as I landed.

I rolled onto my back and sat up. With me, similarly bound, were Charles and the man in the tan coat.

I scooted toward Charles. "You okay?"

"I'm hurt. My arm's broken," he said, his voice straining with pain. "What happened to you?"

"They were waiting for me at the car. I'm sorry."

"Check on the other guy," Charles said.

I scooted toward the other man. His face was a mass of blood and swelling, his eyes covered with tape and his hands bound behind him.

"Can you hear me?" I said softly into his ear.

He didn't reply. His breath was shallow and raspy.

"He's out cold," I said, "but he's still breathing."

"Our only hope is for Julia to call the police and for them to find us before —"

Just then, Paul climbed behind the wheel of the van. Dweezer got in on the other side.

"We've got a mess here, little bro, and you're going to clean it up," Dweezer said ominously.

As Paul started up the van, I strained to see over the two front seats. I spotted a digital clock.

"Damn," I thought. It was three-fifteen, too early for Julia to call the cops.

"What are you looking at?" said Dweezer.

It was then I noticed he was pointing a gun at me.

"Stay down back there. Flat on your back, bitch," he ordered.

I crouched down on the floor. My mind raced. If they took us someplace else, we were doomed. Unless ... Had Julia taken down the plate number on the van or at least the name of the rental agency? If these frat boys were smart, they would have rented it with a stolen credit card and license — child's play for men who had already killed. Still, an alert clerk could identify them by sight.

The video camera, back at my car. Maybe I could use that as a bargaining chip.

* * * * *

As Paul drove the van, I flexed and strained my arms and legs to try to loosen the tape. It was no use. The man who had bound me had done a thorough job.

Even with my wrists and feet bound, I could roll quickly to the van's back doors and jump out. But once I hit the ground, I couldn't run. It would be simple enough for them to stop the van and shoot me or run over me. Besides, I couldn't get all three of us out in time. Flagging down a passing vehicle from inside the van would also prove difficult. The van had no side windows behind the passenger and driver doors and only two small windows on the back.

I had to get my hands on a weapon. The lug wrench! Of course. I looked around. I spotted the jack and tire iron bracketed to the wall on the driver's side just inside the back doors. First I could club Dweezer over the head, even with my hands bound, get the gun, and then force Paul to stop the van.

I looked at Charles, who was lying next to me. Every move of the van produced a new grimace of agony on his sweat-drenched face.

I winked, then put my fingers to my lips for him to be quiet. He nodded, almost imperceptibly.

Moving slowly and quietly, I sat up and turned myself around, the back of my head pointed toward the van's rear doors. I used my legs to push myself backward, all the while keeping my eyes trained on the men in the two seats up front. When I reached the back, I started working on the two large wing nuts holding the bracket in place. The first one came off easily.

I was at work on the second one when Dweezer turned around. "What the fuck do you think you're doing?" he said angrily.

"Just trying to get more comfortable."

"Slide up front where I can keep an eye on you," he said.

I stayed where I was. "What difference does it make? I just want some more space," I said. "I can't go anywhere."

"Don't make me say it again." His tone was murderous.

I did what he said.

After about an hour, the van stopped. Paul and Dweezer got out. Then the back doors opened.

First, they dragged out the beating victim, who was still out cold.

Then they pulled out Charles, who was helpless with pain.

He let out a fierce, wordless cry as they threw him to the ground behind the van.

Then it was my turn. Dweezer and Paul each grabbed an arm and pulled me out of the van. I had no idea where we were, only that we were in a remote, wooded area. The rest of the gang had not followed. Paul and Dweezer threw me to the ground, face down. I landed hard against the frozen dirt. Rolling over onto my back, I watched the two men converse by the van a few feet away.

"You have to do it," Dweezer said to Paul.

"You've got to pull the trigger on at least one of them."

"Dweezer," I said as calmly as I could manage, "I have a videotape of you and your gang beating up this man here. You'll never get away with your crimes, even if you kill us. You can only make it worse for yourself."

He ignored me.

"Nobody in your gang knows where the camera is," I said. "If you kill me, the police will find it first."

"Do it," Dweezer said to Paul. "Your hands are just as dirty as mine, little bro. You've been on every fag run we've made. If I go down, we all go down. Do it!"

Paul shook his head.

"You fucking baby," Dweezer said.

He stalked over to me, bent over and shoved the gun in my face. The barrel touched my nose. "This is how you kill somebody," he said angrily.

"Noooooooo!" Charles screamed.

CHAPTER NINE

Charles's sharp cry stirred me from my memories.

I could smell the gun — oily and metallic. Acid filled my mouth. Dweezer's finger tightened around the trigger. I was going to die.

Nothing happened.

"Fucking safety," he muttered.

I was still alive. Seizing the moment, I rolled back onto my shoulders, pulled my knees toward my chest and kicked him as hard as I could, pushing him away from my body. Dweezer fell backward, the gun flying out of his hand.

"Grab the gun or he'll kill us all," I shouted. "Paul, do something — for Toni's sake."

As Dweezer struggled to right himself, Paul came to life and grabbed the gun, training it on Dweezer.

"That's enough, Dweezer," Paul said. "Enough killing."

"Don't do anything crazy, little bro," he said, walking toward Paul. "If you can't do it, I will. Okay? I'm sorry for what I said."

Paul was shaking. "Don't come any closer, man. I'll fucking kill you."

"You're not going to kill me," he said, calmly and soothingly. He was almost close enough to grab the gun.

"You fucking bastards killed my sister. You killed her," he said, crying.

"We killed her? Why did she show up at the ceremony? You spilled about the fag runs, didn't you, man? I know that. I understand why. You were scared because they kept getting messier, and you told her about them. That's why she was there, trying to stop something that only Sigma men are supposed to know about. You should have come to me to talk about it," he said, his tone conciliatory and understanding, his palms held out in supplication.

"Shut up, man. Just shut the fuck up. I gotta think here," Paul screeched. He was trembling, a wild look on his face.

"Just ask yourself why she was there," Dweezer said quietly. "The person who told her about our Sigma secret rituals is responsible for her death. She didn't belong there."

"Shut up," said Paul, crazy with panic. "I fucking told you to shut up."

"I'm on your side. I've been looking out for you all this time, little bro," he said, his voice almost hypnotic. "You were supposed to hide her body like we did the faggot's. You asked to take care of her body, and I'm the one who said okay. Hey, I'm not blaming you. But you called the police to say where she was. Everyone in the house knows you were the once who called. Everyone in the house knows you told her about our rituals. You brought down the heat on your Sigma brothers. You took an oath, man, and you broke it. I'll be honest with you. Most of the Sigmas wanted to see you dead. You think that planting the bat on Leonard saved you? Yeah, it was a good idea, but I'm the one who kept you alive. I believe in Sigma loyalty, dude."

Frantically gasping for breath, Paul said, "I couldn't leave . . . my sister . . . to just rot . . . like some stray dog . . . by the side of the road."

"Man, I understand. I forgive you. Let me clean up this mess. I'll take care of everything. We'll stand together as Sigmas."

Dweezer inched forward and reached for the gun. Paul pulled the trigger, and Dweezer dropped.

The rest of the night passed in a blur. My only clear memory was driving back to Frontier City at top speed as the wounded moaned with each jolt of the van and as Paul wailed inconsolably.

* * * * *

Sunday morning, I woke up in St. Joseph's Hospital with Julia napping, slumped over in a chair at my bedside. My head pounded from the blows I'd taken the night before and my body ached all over, but, thank God, I was alive.

"Julia," I said quietly.

She awoke as soon as she heard my voice.

"I never thought I'd see you again," I said stretching my hand out to her.

She got up and sat on the bed. When she put her arms around me, something collapsed inside me. I clutched her as the terror of the night before, the gun shoved in my face, played frame by frame through my head. She held me, gently soothing me, as my tears flowed.

"How's Charles?" I asked after I finally had composed myself.

"He's banged up. Multiple fractures on his left arm, abrasions, three broken ribs. But he's going to make it," Julia said. "In fact, I'm taking you both home this afternoon, provided you pass your neurological tests. The doctor was worried about you last night — because of that blow to your head. You weren't making a lot of sense."

"How are the other two guys?"

"The guy who got shot will live. The other guy's pretty bad. Concussion, broken nose, broken ribs. It's going to be a matter of time before they can tell how serious the brain injury is."

"Help me up. It's time to see how badly I'm hurt," I said, bracing myself for the worst. She grabbed my arm and guided me to the bathroom.

The fluorescent lighting accented every hideous

injury on my bruised, scratched, battered face. My right eye was black and nearly swollen shut. "I look like Anthony Quinn in *Requiem for a Heavyweight*," I said.

"You're the most beautiful sight I've ever seen," Julia said, embracing me as her eyes filled with tears. "I called the cops right at three-thirty, but by then you were gone. They couldn't find you. I almost lost you."

"Don't worry," I said, gently touching her face. "I plan to be here with you for a long time. By the way, where's Grandma?"

"In the waiting room. She's been here all night. I called her last night. In the emergency room, you kept asking for her. Don't you remember?"

"No," I said, wiping away a tear.

"We took turns watching over you," Julia said. "She's been civil. It's scary."

"I'm going to go see her," I said, steadying myself against Julia's arm.

"Are you sure? I could bring her in here."

"Yeah. I need to walk. It'll make both of us feel better if I'm on my feet," I said. "Meanwhile, you stay here and call the newspaper. Go all the way to the top. Get Ned Foxworth on the phone. I'm not screwing around with Newman. Tell him I'm going to have a story to dictate for tomorrow's edition as soon as I check out of here."

Though every inch of my body ached, I walked unassisted into the visitors' lounge.

As soon as I saw Grandma, the old woman's face lit up. "My baby," she said, stretching her arms out.

I knew our fight was over.

CHAPTER TEN

The following Monday morning, I was well enough to travel, so I drove to Oklahoma City.

A bitterly cold wind lashed me as I got out of my car at Lakeview Cemetery.

The sight of the headstone shocked me. It hadn't been there the day of the funeral. Its presence made her death seem all the more permanent.

I read the inscription. ANTOINETTE VICTORIA STEWART, 1961–1987, LOVING DAUGHTER AND DEVOTED SISTER.

"And a hero," I said aloud. I placed a bouquet of yellow roses on her grave.

That day, I wrote Faith Brooks a letter, telling her who Toni was, how she had lived and why she had died. Along with the note, I mailed her the heart-shaped box Toni's mother had given me. I hoped it would give her some peace.

Tuesday, I was still stiff and bruised, but I went back to work. Foxworth, the editor in chief of the *Times,* wasn't enthusiastic when I pitched the idea of covering the fraternity case myself.

A tall, thin, silver-haired man in his middle fifties, he had been at the paper's helm for fifteen years. Foxworth leaned back in his oversized red-leather chair. "Carmen, I'd be much more comfortable letting one of our senior investigative writers cover this case," he said. "This complexity of the issues involved demands that a veteran reporter —"

"Excuse me, Ned," I said, "but that's a load of bullshit."

Foxworth looked at me in surprise.

"That's right. I said *bullshit.* Look at my face. Do I look like I had a nice weekend? I risked my life for this story, and you want to give it to someone else?"

Foxworth took a deep breath. "Of course we'll need your input, but you are assigned to the copy desk."

"The copy desk? I'm not going back there. Back when Sargent was in charge, working the desk meant something. He stood up for his editors and rewarded us for good work. But Jerry Newman? The guy's a control freak and a homophobe. He hates my guts. He doesn't let me work on front-page copy, only the back-of-the-book stuff. Plus he gives me the worst schedule. I won't work for him anymore."

"I'm surprised to hear you take this tack, Carmen," Foxworth said quietly.

I leaned toward him. "When I broke the Barrett case, Sargent made sure I got a bonus, a raise and a byline. I didn't even have to ask him. Now all you're offering me is a one-way ticket back to Newman's house of detention."

Foxworth twirled his chair around and looked out the windows of his spacious office. "Carmen, money is tight right now. As of last quarter —"

"This is a huge story, Ned. It's going national and you know it. That's going to boost the paper's circulation and prestige." I took a breath to work up my courage. I'd nearly taken a bullet in the face. I wouldn't spend my remaining time on earth being stepped on. "If you won't let me cover it, maybe *The Herald* will." *The Herald,* always on the brink of collapse, was the other daily in the city. I didn't want to go there. But I would if I had to.

Foxworth swiveled his chair so he could look at me. His eyes narrowed. "I don't like being threatened."

"And I don't like being kicked in the ass," I said.

Foxworth inhaled and then smoothed out his pants leg.

"Let's see how you do on this story," he said.

"This story is going to take weeks, probably

months to develop. You're going to give me the time I need, right?"

"Agreed." He looked at his watch and cleared his throat.

Foxworth was right about one thing. I hadn't done any reporting since my college newspaper days. I wasn't experienced enough to handle a story of this scope on my own. But I wasn't going to let him know that.

"This story needs at least two reporters. I want Terry. She helped me with background, so she knows the case," I said. Terry was the best reporter in the newsroom and I needed her.

He folded his arms and sighed. "Very well."

"The copy desk?"

"I'll see about finding a new assignment for you. I can't guarantee anything," he said, standing up. "Carmen, I have a meeting with the publisher."

"What about the money?"

He opened the door to show me out. "A raise just isn't in the figures. The best I can offer you is a bonus, an extra two weeks' pay."

"All right," I said.

"And now if that's all —"

I stood my ground. "Ned, I want it all in writing."

Foxworth never lost his composure, but he was angrier than I had ever seen him. "I'll have my secretary type it up today."

Wednesday, my first full day on the story, I spent

several hours tracking down information at the courthouse. Then I headed back to the newsroom to go through my notes and work on my story. Meanwhile, Terry, delighted to be assigned another high-profile story, was interviewing the chief detectives on the case.

I was typing furiously when I sensed somebody standing over my desk.

I looked up. It was Newman — more nervous, sweaty and uncomfortable than usual.

"Foxworth just told me about your new assignment," he said. "Don't you think you're a little out of your depth?"

"Jerry, I've got tons of work here to do."

"Well, good luck. Just remember, we can always use you on the copy desk."

A chill ran through me. Not if I have anything to do with it, I thought.

With Terry's help, sorting out the facts was proving easy. Paul Stewart, eager to unburden his conscience, had agreed to cooperate with the District Attorney's office in exchange for immunity on the murder charges.

His detailed statements to investigators provided a picture of how and why Toni and Desmond died.

Disturbed by the escalating violence of his fraternity's "fag runs," Paul first went to his sister for help the day I visited her town house — the day he found out he had been selected to serve on the pledge initiation committee with Dweezer. Toni called him back after I left, but by then, he had decided to clam up.

His anxiety grew as the first scheduled fag run of the school year drew closer. The night before Toni and Desmond died, Paul showed up at his sister's home in a state of hysteria. The following night, he told her, the Sigmas planned to find a gay man at Wilde's, lure him to Cherokee Park and rough him up so badly that afterward "he would be stuck in a wheelchair or a casket."

Toni urged him to call the family's attorney and then to go to the police with what he knew. He refused, worried about facing jail and the wrath of current and former Sigmas once he got out. Toni grew more agitated. Didn't he realize that she was just like the people he was beating up? Stunned and angry that his sister was "queer," Paul stormed out of Toni's place and returned to the Sigma house early that morning.

That night, Toni went to Wilde's, presumably to find Paul, but she never spotted him and he never saw her. He and Dweezer, sitting in a rented van, were waiting for their pledge to pick a victim. Unwilling to contact the police, she called me instead, hoping I could expose the violence without implicating Paul. As she stood outside talking to me on the pay phone, she must have spotted the pledge, too young to get into the bar, inviting Desmond to go to Lake Sequoyah. She cut short the call and followed the gang to the park.

There, she witnessed Desmond Allen's savage beating. She stepped out of the shadows and demanded that the gang stop. As the men circled her and she realized the danger she was in, she cried out, "Paul, tell them I'm your sister." Paul begged his frat brothers to let her go. Dweezer shook his head, condemning Toni to death. Held down by two men, Paul watched as the Sigmas brutally murdered his sister and then the badly injured Desmond Allen.

Afterwards, the Sigmas were ready to turn on Paul. But he kept himself alive by suggesting a brilliant idea — Leonard Martin could easily be framed for the murders should the bodies ever be found. He himself would take care of planting the evidence.

Dweezer and his buddies took care of hiding Desmond's body under a tarp and some brush. Paul insisted that he be left alone to handle his sister's remains.

Deciding to weigh down her pockets with rocks and then throw her into the lake, he dragged her to the water's edge. After gathering several large rocks, he looked down at her battered, lifeless body. He screamed in terror, but no one heard him. He dragged her back into the woods and then ran away, crying, shouting and wishing he were dead. By the time he met the rest of the Sigmas back at the parking lot, he was numb. He assured them Toni's body would never be found. Believing his story, the Sigmas took off into the night.

That weekend, Paul Stewart went to his parents' home to escape his guilt. But his conscience tortured him as he watched his parents worry over their daughter's disappearance, as he looked at Toni's pictures on the mantel and as he walked in the yard where he and his big sister had played as children.

When he got back to town the next week, he

made a decision. He couldn't bring his sister back, but he could give his parents some peace. From a pay phone, he called police to tell them the location of Toni's body.

He hoped the guilt would subside.

But it didn't.

Meanwhile, the Sigmas grew hostile and suspicious when Toni's body showed up so quickly. Paul grew more withdrawn, haunted by his guilt.

Then my friends and I started digging around. Paul saw a way out. Hoping I could stop the madness, he sent me the anonymous note.

Through Paul's testimony before a grand jury, our videotape, eyewitness accounts from me, Charles and, amazingly, Bill Ryan, the beating victim we rescued, thirty-two current members of Sigma Alpha Sigma were to stand trial on charges of murder and assault. Some sixty former members were also to stand trial on assault charges.

Ryan, an insurance agent from Joplin, Missouri, was making a steady recovery from his massive head injuries.

Fifteen victims, once afraid of police indifference, also came forward to testify about the abuse they suffered at the hands of Sigma Alpha Sigma members.

Promised lenience by the district attorney, many current and former members of the fraternity came forward to tell their stories.

FCU's Sigma Alpha Sigmas had once been content to initiate pledges at a midnight candlelight ceremony after paddling, humiliating and bullying them for weeks.

The AIDS crisis and the success of the gay rights

movement changed all that. Homophobia, always a given in this conservative Bible Belt campus, gradually grew.

The first steps toward violence started in the early Eighties. Individual members banded together to shout insults at patrons leaving the city's men's bars. Soon, the members grew bored with mere verbal harassment. By 1982, many Sigmas were routinely roughing up gay men. And by the spring of 1985, hunting down gay men on "fag runs" had become a routine form of recreation for most of FCU's Sigmas. Still, some men balked at taking part in the violence. Taking a secret vote the following fall, the chapter made it a matter of policy — without taking part in a "fag run," a pledge would not be accepted into Sigma Alpha Sigma.

Prosecutors estimated that upwards of one hundred gay men had been assaulted over the five-year period.

The case proved to be a massive embarrassment. Many of the defendants were members of important families. And most of the alumni were well on their way to building prominent careers in business and government. Even a U.S. senator's son was involved.

The national governing body of Sigma Alpha Sigma revoked the FCU chapter's charter. The university, reeling from the bad publicity, also withdrew the fraternity's standing as a student organization.

Donald "Dweezer" Oldfield recovered quickly from a gunshot wound to the abdomen. He was being held without bail at the Frontier City/County Jail on charges of murder, conspiracy to commit murder, attempted murder, assault, kidnapping and illegal weapons possession.

While the facts of this case fell easily into place, the reason for this hatred eluded me. I had spent my whole life resisting the pressure to conform. The idea of giving up individual responsibility in order to belong to a mindless, vicious pack was incomprehensible to me.

I found myself thinking about what Grandma had told me the morning I was in the hospital.

"What makes people act like that?" I asked her in the visitors' lounge. "What makes them want to torture and kill others, just because somebody tells them to do it? What happens to their ability to think for themselves?"

As so often was the case, Grandma turned to the Bible for her answer. "Back in the days of the Apostles," she said, "the religious bigwigs told Peter and the rest of the Disciples to stop teaching what they had learned firsthand from Jesus, what they had seen with their own eyes. Do you remember how Peter answered them?"

I nodded, recalling the passage from the book of Acts. " 'We ought to obey God rather than men,' " I said.

"That's your answer," she said. "It's just like what happened with those old Nazis in Germany, falling all over themselves to wave those flags, beat those drums and give those stupid salutes, all in the name of obeying Hitler."

I looked at her. "I think you're right."

A wicked look came over Grandma's face. "You know, Carmen, we should have wiped all those German bastards off the face of the Earth when we had the chance." As far as Grandma was concerned, we were still at war with the Axis. She wasn't about to forgive or forget.

Mrs. Stewart ordered a glass of chardonnay as we waited for our lunch orders of sole and asparagus to arrive. It was late March.

"Do please order a glass of wine, dear," said Mrs. Stewart, who was treating me to lunch at the restaurant of the swank Frontier Plaza hotel downtown. She was staying there to keep up with the fraternity murder case, to visit her son in jail and to supervise the sale of Toni's town house. Though she looked elegant in her dark blue wool pantsuit and yellow silk blouse, her long ordeal had taken a toll on her appearance. She looked tired and sad.

"No thanks," I said. "I'm working today. How's Bradley?"

"He's doing his best to put his life back together. He comes to see me from time to time."

"And Paul?" Toni's brother had declined my many requests to meet with him.

"They've got him on suicide watch," she said, looking into her glass of wine. "He's devastated. He's not eating, not sleeping."

"Mr. Stewart?"

"David wants nothing to do with Paul or me. He stays in his office and buries himself in his work. It's just as well anyway. He's no good to me, to Paul, even to himself." Mrs. Stewart's face sagged with despair. "I don't know what to do. Losing my children has made me feel how really alone I am."

"At least your son has a conscience. He tried to stop the beatings by telling Toni. He helped me solve two murders. And he saved three lives, Louise, including mine. And he prevented countless more assaults," I said. "And don't ever forget that Toni is a great hero. She couldn't have been that without you."

She reached across the table and patted my hand. "It's the only thing that keeps me going," she said wearily.

It was Sunday in early April. "We want you to come to dinner next Sunday evening." I had been on the phone with Grandma for five minutes before I worked up the courage to ask.

"Where's that fellow going to be?"

"Charles? He's leaving for California tomorrow morning." He had to get back to campus so he could review his research with his dissertation adviser before the term ended.

She said nothing.

"You know, there's a biblical precedent for eating with sinners. Jesus Himself ate with the prostitutes and tax collectors. We can't be any worse than that. Come on, old girl. Loosen up."

I heard a strange sound coming from her. She was actually chuckling. "Okay. All right. You got me. What time?"

"Six o'clock sharp."

"I'll miss evening worship. Brother Rex is preaching on the book of Revelation."

"Come on. Don't you have it memorized by now? All that stuff about the Four Horsemen of the Apocalypse, the Beast, the False Prophet, the Whore of Babylon must be old hat for you by now."

"God's Word is eternal and everlasting truth."

"So it will hold over for one week. I'm making meatloaf and mashed potatoes and brown gravy."

"All right," she said, "but I'm bringing a peach cobbler."

Monday was a typical early April day. Greenish-purple clouds raced across the sky. A heavy downpour was imminent. Julia and I were helping Charles load the last of his suitcases into his Toyota Tercel for the trip to Berkeley when the phone rang.

"Carmen, it's been a really bad day. I need to talk," Leonard Martin said, his voice slow, as if he just woke up.

"Okay," I said with a sigh. "But just for a minute. I'm really busy." Instead of thanking me or offering me a token of gratitude — like dinner, a bottle of expensive champagne, or movie passes — Leonard Martin had made me his therapist. At least three times a week since he had been freed from jail in mid-February, Leonard called me. As soon as I picked up the phone, he was off and running for hours at a time, talking in mind-numbing detail about his problems. Initially, I was sympathetic as he recounted his ordeal behind bars, lonely upbringing, friendless existence and lingering obsession for Charles. But lately, I was starting to feel like a coyote in a leg-hold trap.

"Is Charles still in town? Can I talk to him? Just for a minute, just to say goodbye?" he asked.

Charles and Julia had followed me into the house when the phone rang. I pointed at the phone and mouthed the word "Leonard" at Charles, who had steadfastly avoided all contact with him for months. Charles shook his head vigorously.

"As a matter of fact, he left early this morning for California," I said.

"Do you have his address out there?"

"Leonard, forget about him. Get some help for yourself. Please."

"It could work with him. I know it," Leonard said.

I had nothing left to say.

"Well, I guess I'll see you at the next coalition meeting. Won't I?"

"Yes, Leonard, but I've got to go now."

Julia, Tom, Donna and Leonard had re-formed the group after Leonard was freed from jail. And with the fraternity murders dominating the headlines, more gay, lesbian and bisexual students were willing to come out and get involved. Ten people had showed up for the last meeting. I'd been helping them with publicity. Running into Leonard at the meetings was always tough, though. He inevitably tried to turn the gatherings into therapy sessions. He was wearing me and the members of the group out.

"Three-and-a-half-months in jail, Carmen. Do you know what that's like? Nobody believed me. Especially not you —"

My face got hot. "Leonard, stop that. You're being manipulative and I don't like that. Now I've got to go. Goodbye." I hung up. Seconds later, the phone rang again. I unplugged it.

Planting my hands on my hips, I scowled at Julia. "If I had five minutes to live, this guy would spend four minutes and fifty-nine seconds telling me how miserable he is."

Julia shrugged. "He's got a lot of problems."

"Then, for God's sake, let him get a shrink. He's imprinted on me, like a baby duck. You've got to get this guy off me."

"I will. I promise," she said. "I'll call the campus psych center tomorrow and get a couple of referrals for him."

"You couldn't arrange for a heavy sedation and a long stay at a state mental health hospital?" I asked.

Julia laughed.

I turned to Charles. "And that's the last lie I tell for you, pal."

"You didn't lie. It was almost true. I wanted to leave early this morning. Besides, I'm horrible with goodbyes," he said, adjusting his yellow "Cat" baseball hat and then zipping up his blue windbreaker, which advertised Zebco fishing tackle. Stuffed in his coat pocket was Bucky, the lavender stuffed rabbit Julia and I had given him that Easter, which had fallen in late March that year.

"I'm not great at them either," I said, tears filling my eyes.

"You like my ensemble?" he said, twirling like a fashion model on a runway. "I like to go butch when I'm on the road."

"Yes, you're totally butch, a veritable Mr.

Testosterone, especially with that rabbit," I said. "Oh why can't Leonard go to California? You stay here instead."

"You know I can't," he said softly. He hugged me and Julia and then headed for the door.

"Julia, goodbye, my dear," he said. "Force Ms. Paranoid to bring you out to California for a visit, will you? That is, if you can pry Leonard off her. We don't have earthquakes every day and the Zodiac Killer has been inactive for quite some time."

"I will," she said, crying for the umpteenth time that morning. "You sure you don't want to stay on as our houseboy?"

"It's a very appealing offer." He wiped away a tear and turned to me. "And Carmen, you take good care of Julia."

"I will," I said. "I promise."

"Both of you, remember how lucky you are," he said.

Julia and I followed Charles onto the front porch. The storm that had threatened was now gone. Blue sky and sunlight broke through the clouds.

Charles held up the little lavender rabbit, waved its stuffed paw at us and then got in the car.

Arm in arm, we watched him drive away, heading west.

A few of the publications of
THE NAIAD PRESS, INC.
P.O. Box 10543 • Tallahassee, Florida 32302
Phone (904) 539-5965
Toll-Free Order Number: 1-800-533-1973
Mail orders welcome. Please include 15% postage.

FINAL CUT by Lisa Haddock. 208 pp. A Carmen Ramirez mystery.
ISBN 1-56280-088-4 $10.95

FLASHPOINT by Katherine V. Forrest. 256 pp. A Lesbian
blockbuster!   ISBN 1-56280-079-5   10.95

DAUGHTERS OF A CORAL DAWN by Katherine V. Forrest.
Audio Book — read by Jane Merrow.   ISBN 1-56280-110-4   16.95

CLAIRE OF THE MOON by Nicole Conn. Audio Book —Read
by Marianne Hyatt.   ISBN 1-56280-113-9   16.95

FOR LOVE AND FOR LIFE: INTIMATE PORTRAITS OF
LESBIAN COUPLES by Susan Johnson. 224 pp.
ISBN 1-56280-091-4   14.95

DEVOTION by Mindy Kaplan. 192 pp. See the movie — read
the book!   ISBN 1-56280-093-0   10.95

SOMEONE TO WATCH by Jaye Maiman. 272 pp. A Robin Miller
mystery. 4th in a series.   ISBN 1-56280-095-7   10.95

GREENER THAN GRASS by Jennifer Fulton. 208 pp. A young
woman — a stranger in her bed.   ISBN 1-56280-092-2   10.95

TRAVELS WITH DIANA HUNTER by Regine Sands. Erotic
lesbian romp. Audio Book (2 cassettes)   ISBN 1-56280-107-4   16.95

CABIN FEVER by Carol Schmidt. 256 pp. Sizzling suspense
and passion.   ISBN 1-56280-089-1   10.95

THERE WILL BE NO GOODBYES by Laura DeHart Young. 192
pp. Romantic love, strength, and friendship.   ISBN 1-56280-103-1   10.95

FAULTLINE by Sheila Ortiz Taylor. 144 pp. Joyous comic
lesbian novel.   ISBN 1-56280-108-2   9.95

OPEN HOUSE by Pat Welch. 176 pp. P.I. Helen Black's fourth
case.   ISBN 1-56280-102-3   10.95

ONCE MORE WITH FEELING by Peggy J. Herring. 240 pp.
Lighthearted, loving romantic adventure.   ISBN 1-56280-089-2   10.95

FOREVER by Evelyn Kennedy. 224 pp. Passionate romance — love
overcoming all obstacles.   ISBN 1-56280-094-9   10.95

WHISPERS by Kris Bruyer. 176 pp. Romantic ghost story
ISBN 1-56280-082-5   10.95

NIGHT SONGS by Penny Mickelbury. 224 pp. A Gianna
Maglione Mystery. Second in a series.   ISBN 1-56280-097-3   10.95

GETTING TO THE POINT by Teresa Stores. 256 pp. Classic
southern Lesbian novel.   ISBN 1-56280-100-7   10.95

PAINTED MOON by Karin Kallmaker. 224 pp. Delicious
Kallmaker romance.   ISBN 1-56280-075-2   9.95

THE MYSTERIOUS NAIAD edited by Katherine V. Forrest &
Barbara Grier. 320 pp. Love stories by Naiad Press authors.
ISBN 1-56280-074-4   14.95

DAUGHTERS OF A CORAL DAWN by Katherine V. Forrest.
240 pp. Tenth Anniversay Edition.   ISBN 1-56280-104-X   10.95

BODY GUARD by Claire McNab. 208 pp. A Carol Ashton Mystery.
6th in a series.   ISBN 1-56280-073-6   10.95

CACTUS LOVE by Lee Lynch. 192 pp. Stories by the beloved
storyteller.   ISBN 1-56280-071-X   9.95

SECOND GUESS by Rose Beecham. 216 pp. An Amanda Valentine
Mystery. 2nd in a series.   ISBN 1-56280-069-8   9.95

THE SURE THING by Melissa Hartman. 208 pp. L.A. earthquake
romance.   ISBN 1-56280-078-7   9.95

A RAGE OF MAIDENS by Lauren Wright Douglas. 240 pp. A
Caitlin Reece Mystery. 6th in a series.   ISBN 1-56280-068-X   10.95

TRIPLE EXPOSURE by Jackie Calhoun. 224 pp. Romantic drama
involving many characters.   ISBN 1-56280-067-1   9.95

UP, UP AND AWAY by Catherine Ennis. 192 pp. Delightful
romance.   ISBN 1-56280-065-5   9.95

PERSONAL ADS by Robbi Sommers. 176 pp. Sizzling short
stories.   ISBN 1-56280-059-0   9.95

FLASHPOINT by Katherine V. Forrest. 256 pp. Lesbian
blockbuster!   ISBN 1-56280-043-4   22.95

CROSSWORDS by Penny Sumner. 256 pp. 2nd Victoria Cross
Mystery.   ISBN 1-56280-064-7   9.95

SWEET CHERRY WINE by Carol Schmidt. 224 pp. A novel of
suspense.   ISBN 1-56280-063-9   9.95

CERTAIN SMILES by Dorothy Tell. 160 pp. Erotic short stories.
ISBN 1-56280-066-3   9.95

EDITED OUT by Lisa Haddock. 224 pp. 1st Carmen Ramirez
Mystery.   ISBN 1-56280-077-9   9.95

WEDNESDAY NIGHTS by Camarin Grae. 288 pp. Sexy
adventure.   ISBN 1-56280-060-4   10.95

SMOKEY O by Celia Cohen. 176 pp. Relationships on the playing field. ISBN 1-56280-057-4   9.95

KATHLEEN O'DONALD by Penny Hayes. 256 pp. Rose and Kathleen find each other and employment in 1909 NYC.
ISBN 1-56280-070-1   9.95

STAYING HOME by Elisabeth Nonas. 256 pp. Molly and Alix want a baby . . . or do they?   ISBN 1-56280-076-0   10.95

TRUE LOVE by Jennifer Fulton. 240 pp. Six lesbians searching for love in all the "right" places.   ISBN 1-56280-035-3   9.95

GARDENIAS WHERE THERE ARE NONE by Molleen Zanger. 176 pp. Why is Melanie inextricably drawn to the old house?
ISBN 1-56280-056-6   9.95

KEEPING SECRETS by Penny Mickelbury. 208 pp. A Gianna Maglione Mystery. First in a series.   ISBN 1-56280-052-3   9.95

THE ROMANTIC NAIAD edited by Katherine V. Forrest & Barbara Grier. 336 pp. Love stories by Naiad Press authors.
ISBN 1-56280-054-X   14.95

UNDER MY SKIN by Jaye Maiman. 336 pp. A Robin Miller mystery. 3rd in a series.   ISBN 1-56280-049-3.   10.95

STAY TOONED by Rhonda Dicksion. 144 pp. Cartoons — 1st collection since *Lesbian Survival Manual.*   ISBN 1-56280-045-0   9.95

CAR POOL by Karin Kallmaker. 272pp. Lesbians on wheels and then some!   ISBN 1-56280-048-5   9.95

NOT TELLING MOTHER: STORIES FROM A LIFE by Diane Salvatore. 176 pp. Her 3rd novel.   ISBN 1-56280-044-2   9.95

GOBLIN MARKET by Lauren Wright Douglas. 240pp. A Caitlin Reece Mystery. 5th in a series.   ISBN 1-56280-047-7   10.95

LONG GOODBYES by Nikki Baker. 256 pp. A Virginia Kelly mystery. 3rd in a series.   ISBN 1-56280-042-6   9.95

FRIENDS AND LOVERS by Jackie Calhoun. 224 pp. Mid-western Lesbian lives and loves.   ISBN 1-56280-041-8   10.95

THE CAT CAME BACK by Hilary Mullins. 208 pp. Highly praised Lesbian novel.   ISBN 1-56280-040-X   9.95

BEHIND CLOSED DOORS by Robbi Sommers. 192 pp. Hot, erotic short stories.   ISBN 1-56280-039-6   9.95

CLAIRE OF THE MOON by Nicole Conn. 192 pp. See the movie — read the book!   ISBN 1-56280-038-8   10.95

SILENT HEART by Claire McNab. 192 pp. Exotic Lesbian romance.   ISBN 1-56280-036-1   10.95

HAPPY ENDINGS by Kate Brandt. 272 pp. Intimate conversations with Lesbian authors.   ISBN 1-56280-050-7   10.95

THE SPY IN QUESTION by Amanda Kyle Williams. 256 pp.
4th Madison McGuire.   ISBN 1-56280-037-X   9.95

SAVING GRACE by Jennifer Fulton. 240 pp. Adventure and
romantic entanglement.   ISBN 1-56280-051-5   9.95

THE YEAR SEVEN by Molleen Zanger. 208 pp. Women surviving
in a new world.   ISBN 1-56280-034-5   9.95

CURIOUS WINE by Katherine V. Forrest. 176 pp. Tenth Anniver-
sary Edition. The most popular contemporary Lesbian love story.
                                        ISBN 1-56280-053-1   10.95
        Audio Book (2 cassettes)   ISBN 1-56280-105-8   16.95

CHAUTAUQUA by Catherine Ennis. 192 pp. Exciting, romantic
adventure.   ISBN 1-56280-032-9   9.95

A PROPER BURIAL by Pat Welch. 192 pp. A Helen Black
mystery. 3rd in a series.   ISBN 1-56280-033-7   9.95

SILVERLAKE HEAT: A Novel of Suspense by Carol Schmidt.
240 pp. Rhonda is as hot as Laney's dreams.   ISBN 1-56280-031-0   9.95

LOVE, ZENA BETH by Diane Salvatore. 224 pp. The most talked
about lesbian novel of the nineties!   ISBN 1-56280-030-2   10.95

A DOORYARD FULL OF FLOWERS by Isabel Miller. 160 pp.
Stories incl. 2 sequels to *Patience and Sarah.*   ISBN 1-56280-029-9   9.95

MURDER BY TRADITION by Katherine V. Forrest. 288 pp. A
Kate Delafield Mystery. 4th in a series.   ISBN 1-56280-002-7   10.95

THE EROTIC NAIAD edited by Katherine V. Forrest & Barbara
Grier. 224 pp. Love stories by Naiad Press authors.
                                        ISBN 1-56280-026-4   13.95

DEAD CERTAIN by Claire McNab. 224 pp. A Carol Ashton
mystery. 5th in a series.   ISBN 1-56280-027-2   9.95

CRAZY FOR LOVING by Jaye Maiman. 320 pp. A Robin Miller
mystery. 2nd in a series.   ISBN 1-56280-025-6   9.95

STONEHURST by Barbara Johnson. 176 pp. Passionate regency
romance.   ISBN 1-56280-024-8   9.95

INTRODUCING AMANDA VALENTINE by Rose Beecham.
256 pp. An Amanda Valentine Mystery. First in a series.
                                        ISBN 1-56280-021-3   9.95

UNCERTAIN COMPANIONS by Robbi Sommers. 204 pp.
Steamy, erotic novel.   ISBN 1-56280-017-5   9.95

A TIGER'S HEART by Lauren W. Douglas. 240 pp. A Caitlin
Reece mystery. 4th in a series.   ISBN 1-56280-018-3   9.95

PAPERBACK ROMANCE by Karin Kallmaker. 256 pp. A
delicious romance.   ISBN 1-56280-019-1   9.95

MORTON RIVER VALLEY by Lee Lynch. 304 pp. Lee Lynch
at her best!   ISBN 1-56280-016-7   9.95

THE LAVENDER HOUSE MURDER by Nikki Baker. 224 pp.
A Virginia Kelly Mystery. 2nd in a series.   ISBN 1-56280-012-4   9.95

PASSION BAY by Jennifer Fulton. 224 pp. Passionate romance,
virgin beaches, tropical skies.   ISBN 1-56280-028-0   10.95

STICKS AND STONES by Jackie Calhoun. 208 pp. Contemporary
lesbian lives and loves.   ISBN 1-56280-020-5   9.95
Audio Book (2 cassettes)   ISBN 1-56280-106-6   16.95

DELIA IRONFOOT by Jeane Harris. 192 pp. Adventure for Delia
and Beth in the Utah mountains.   ISBN 1-56280-014-0   9.95

UNDER THE SOUTHERN CROSS by Claire McNab. 192 pp.
Romantic nights Down Under.   ISBN 1-56280-011-6   9.95

GRASSY FLATS by Penny Hayes. 256 pp. Lesbian romance in
the '30s.   ISBN 1-56280-010-8   9.95

A SINGULAR SPY by Amanda K. Williams. 192 pp. 3rd
Madison McGuire.   ISBN 1-56280-008-6   8.95

THE END OF APRIL by Penny Sumner. 240 pp. A Victoria
Cross mystery. First in a series.   ISBN 1-56280-007-8   8.95

HOUSTON TOWN by Deborah Powell. 208 pp. A Hollis
Carpenter mystery.   ISBN 1-56280-006-X   8.95

KISS AND TELL by Robbi Sommers. 192 pp. Scorching stories
by the author of *Pleasures*.   ISBN 1-56280-005-1   10.95

STILL WATERS by Pat Welch. 208 pp. A Helen Black mystery.
2nd in a series.   ISBN 0-941483-97-5   9.95

TO LOVE AGAIN by Evelyn Kennedy. 208 pp. Wildly romantic
love story.   ISBN 0-941483-85-1   9.95

IN THE GAME by Nikki Baker. 192 pp. A Virginia Kelly
mystery. First in a series.   ISBN 1-56280-004-3   9.95

AVALON by Mary Jane Jones. 256 pp. A Lesbian Arthurian
romance.   ISBN 0-941483-96-7   9.95

STRANDED by Camarin Grae. 320 pp. Entertaining, riveting
adventure.   ISBN 0-941483-99-1   9.95

THE DAUGHTERS OF ARTEMIS by Lauren Wright Douglas.
240 pp. A Caitlin Reece mystery. 3rd in a series.
     ISBN 0-941483-95-9   9.95

CLEARWATER by Catherine Ennis. 176 pp. Romantic secrets
of a small Louisiana town.   ISBN 0-941483-65-7   8.95

THE HALLELUJAH MURDERS by Dorothy Tell. 176 pp. A
Poppy Dillworth mystery. 2nd in a series.   ISBN 0-941483-88-6   8.95

SECOND CHANCE by Jackie Calhoun. 256 pp. Contemporary
Lesbian lives and loves.   ISBN 0-941483-93-2   9.95

BENEDICTION by Diane Salvatore. 272 pp. Striking, contemporary romantic novel.   ISBN 0-941483-90-8   9.95

BLACK IRIS by Jeane Harris. 192 pp. Caroline's hidden past . . .
ISBN 0-941483-68-1   8.95

TOUCHWOOD by Karin Kallmaker. 240 pp. Loving, May/
December romance.   ISBN 0-941483-76-2   9.95

COP OUT by Claire McNab. 208 pp. A Carol Ashton mystery.
4th in a series.   ISBN 0-941483-84-3   9.95

THE BEVERLY MALIBU by Katherine V. Forrest. 288 pp. A
Kate Delafield Mystery. 3rd in a series.   ISBN 0-941483-48-7   10.95

THAT OLD STUDEBAKER by Lee Lynch. 272 pp. Andy's affair
with Regina and her attachment to her beloved car.
ISBN 0-941483-82-7   9.95

PASSION'S LEGACY by Lori Paige. 224 pp. Sarah is swept into
the arms of Augusta Pym in this delightful historical romance.
ISBN 0-941483-81-9   8.95

THE PROVIDENCE FILE by Amanda Kyle Williams. 256 pp.
Second Madison McGuire   ISBN 0-941483-92-4   8.95

I LEFT MY HEART by Jaye Maiman. 320 pp. A Robin Miller
Mystery. First in a series.   ISBN 0-941483-72-X   10.95

THE PRICE OF SALT by Patricia Highsmith (writing as Claire
Morgan). 288 pp. Classic lesbian novel, first issued in 1952 . . .
acknowledged by its author under her own, very famous, name.
ISBN 1-56280-003-5   9.95

SIDE BY SIDE by Isabel Miller. 256 pp. From beloved author of
Patience and Sarah.   ISBN 0-941483-77-0   9.95

STAYING POWER: LONG TERM LESBIAN COUPLES by
Susan E. Johnson. 352 pp. Joys of coupledom. ISBN 0-941-483-75-4   14.95

SLICK by Camarin Grae. 304 pp. Exotic, erotic adventure.
ISBN 0-941483-74-6   9.95

NINTH LIFE by Lauren Wright Douglas. 256 pp. A Caitlin Reece
mystery. 2nd in a series.   ISBN 0-941483-50-9   8.95

PLAYERS by Robbi Sommers. 192 pp. Sizzling, erotic novel.
ISBN 0-941483-73-8   9.95

MURDER AT RED ROOK RANCH by Dorothy Tell. 224 pp.
A Poppy Dillworth mystery. 1st in a series.   ISBN 0-941483-80-0   8.95

LESBIAN SURVIVAL MANUAL by Rhonda Dicksion. 112 pp.
Cartoons!   ISBN 0-941483-71-1   8.95

A ROOM FULL OF WOMEN by Elisabeth Nonas. 256 pp.
Contemporary Lesbian lives.   ISBN 0-941483-69-X   9.95

THEME FOR DIVERSE INSTRUMENTS by Jane Rule. 208 pp.
Powerful romantic lesbian stories.   ISBN 0-941483-63-0   8.95

CLUB 12 by Amanda Kyle Williams. 288 pp. Espionage thriller
featuring a lesbian agent!   ISBN 0-941483-64-9   8.95

DEATH DOWN UNDER by Claire McNab. 240 pp. A Carol
Ashton mystery. 3rd in a series.   ISBN 0-941483-39-8   9.95

MONTANA FEATHERS by Penny Hayes. 256 pp. Vivian and
Elizabeth find love in frontier Montana.   ISBN 0-941483-61-4   8.95

LIFESTYLES by Jackie Calhoun. 224 pp. Contemporary Lesbian
lives and loves.   ISBN 0-941483-57-6   9.95

WILDERNESS TREK by Dorothy Tell. 192 pp. Six women on
vacation learning ''new'' skills.   ISBN 0-941483-60-6   8.95

MURDER BY THE BOOK by Pat Welch. 256 pp. A Helen Black
Mystery. First in a series.   ISBN 0-941483-59-2   9.95

THERE'S SOMETHING I'VE BEEN MEANING TO TELL YOU
Ed. by Loralee MacPike. 288 pp. Gay men and lesbians coming out
to their children.   ISBN 0-941483-44-4   9.95

LIFTING BELLY by Gertrude Stein. Ed. by Rebecca Mark. 104 pp.
Erotic poetry.   ISBN 0-941483-51-7   10.95

AFTER THE FIRE by Jane Rule. 256 pp. Warm, human novel by
this incomparable author.   ISBN 0-941483-45-2   8.95

THREE WOMEN by March Hastings. 232 pp. Golden oldie. A
triangle among wealthy sophisticates.   ISBN 0-941483-43-6   8.95

PLEASURES by Robbi Sommers. 204 pp. Unprecedented
eroticism.   ISBN 0-941483-49-5   8.95

EDGEWISE by Camarin Grae. 372 pp. Spellbinding
adventure.   ISBN 0-941483-19-3   9.95

FATAL REUNION by Claire McNab. 224 pp. A Carol Ashton
mystery. 2nd in a series.   ISBN 0-941483-40-1   8.95

IN EVERY PORT by Karin Kallmaker. 228 pp. Jessica's sexy,
adventuresome travels.   ISBN 0-941483-37-7   9.95

OF LOVE AND GLORY by Evelyn Kennedy. 192 pp. Exciting
WWII romance.   ISBN 0-941483-32-0   8.95

CLICKING STONES by Nancy Tyler Glenn. 288 pp. Love
transcending time.   ISBN 0-941483-31-2   9.95

SOUTH OF THE LINE by Catherine Ennis. 216 pp. Civil War
adventure.   ISBN 0-941483-29-0   8.95

WOMAN PLUS WOMAN by Dolores Klaich. 300 pp. Supurb
Lesbian overview.   ISBN 0-941483-28-2   9.95

THE FINER GRAIN by Denise Ohio. 216 pp. Brilliant young
college lesbian novel.   ISBN 0-941483-11-8   8.95

OCTOBER OBSESSION by Meredith More. Josie's rich, secret
Lesbian life.   ISBN 0-941483-18-5   8.95

BEFORE STONEWALL: THE MAKING OF A GAY AND
LESBIAN COMMUNITY by Andrea Weiss & Greta Schiller.
96 pp., 25 illus.   ISBN 0-941483-20-7   7.95

OSTEN'S BAY by Zenobia N. Vole. 204 pp. Sizzling adventure
romance set on Bonaire. ISBN 0-941483-15-0 8.95

LESSONS IN MURDER by Claire McNab. 216 pp. A Carol
Ashton mystery. First in a series. ISBN 0-941483-14-2 9.95

YELLOWTHROAT by Penny Hayes. 240 pp. Margarita, bandit,
kidnaps Julia. ISBN 0-941483-10-X 8.95

SAPPHISTRY: THE BOOK OF LESBIAN SEXUALITY by
Pat Califia. 3d edition, revised. 208 pp. ISBN 0-941483-24-X 10.95

CHERISHED LOVE by Evelyn Kennedy. 192 pp. Erotic Lesbian
love story. ISBN 0-941483-08-8 10.95

THE SECRET IN THE BIRD by Camarin Grae. 312 pp. Striking,
psychological suspense novel. ISBN 0-941483-05-3 8.95

TO THE LIGHTNING by Catherine Ennis. 208 pp. Romantic
Lesbian 'Robinson Crusoe' adventure. ISBN 0-941483-06-1 8.95

DREAMS AND SWORDS by Katherine V. Forrest. 192 pp.
Romantic, erotic, imaginative stories. ISBN 0-941483-03-7 8.95

MEMORY BOARD by Jane Rule. 336 pp. Memorable novel
about an aging Lesbian couple. ISBN 0-941483-02-9 10.95

THE ALWAYS ANONYMOUS BEAST by Lauren Wright Douglas.
224 pp. A Caitlin Reece mystery. First in a series.
ISBN 0-941483-04-5 8.95

PARENTS MATTER by Ann Muller. 240 pp. Parents' relationships with Lesbian daughters and gay sons. ISBN 0-930044-91-6 9.95

THE BLACK AND WHITE OF IT by Ann Allen Shockley.
144 pp. Short stories. ISBN 0-930044-96-7 7.95

SAY JESUS AND COME TO ME by Ann Allen Shockley. 288
pp. Contemporary romance. ISBN 0-930044-98-3 8.95

MURDER AT THE NIGHTWOOD BAR by Katherine V. Forrest.
240 pp. A Kate Delafield mystery. Second in a series.
ISBN 0-930044-92-4 10.95

WINGED DANCER by Camarin Grae. 228 pp. Erotic Lesbian
adventure story. ISBN 0-930044-88-6 8.95

PAZ by Camarin Grae. 336 pp. Romantic Lesbian adventurer
with the power to change the world. ISBN 0-930044-89-4 8.95

SOUL SNATCHER by Camarin Grae. 224 pp. A puzzle, an
adventure, a mystery — Lesbian romance. ISBN 0-930044-90-8 8.95

THE LOVE OF GOOD WOMEN by Isabel Miller. 224 pp.
Long-awaited new novel by the author of the beloved *Patience
and Sarah.* ISBN 0-930044-81-9 8.95

THE HOUSE AT PELHAM FALLS by Brenda Weathers. 240
pp. Suspenseful Lesbian ghost story. ISBN 0-930044-79-7 7.95

HOME IN YOUR HANDS by Lee Lynch. 240 pp. More stories
from the author of *Old Dyke Tales*.   ISBN 0-930044-80-0   7.95

PEMBROKE PARK by Michelle Martin. 256 pp. Derring-do
and daring romance in Regency England.   ISBN 0-930044-77-0   7.95

THE LONG TRAIL by Penny Hayes. 248 pp. Vivid adventures
of two women in love in the old west.   ISBN 0-930044-76-2   8.95

AN EMERGENCE OF GREEN by Katherine V. Forrest. 288
pp. Powerful novel of sexual discovery.   ISBN 0-930044-69-X   9.95

THE LESBIAN PERIODICALS INDEX edited by Claire Potter.
432 pp. Author & subject index.   ISBN 0-930044-74-6   12.95

DESERT OF THE HEART by Jane Rule. 224 pp. A classic;
basis for the movie *Desert Hearts*.   ISBN 0-930044-73-8   10.95

TORCHLIGHT TO VALHALLA by Gale Wilhelm. 128 pp.
Classic novel by a great Lesbian writer.   ISBN 0-930044-68-1   7.95

LESBIAN NUNS: BREAKING SILENCE edited by Rosemary
Curb and Nancy Manahan. 432 pp. Unprecedented autobiographies
of religious life.   ISBN 0-930044-62-2   9.95

THE SWASHBUCKLER by Lee Lynch. 288 pp. Colorful novel
set in Greenwich Village in the sixties.   ISBN 0-930044-66-5   8.95

SEX VARIANT WOMEN IN LITERATURE by Jeannette
Howard Foster. 448 pp. Literary history.   ISBN 0-930044-65-7   8.95

A HOT-EYED MODERATE by Jane Rule. 252 pp. Hard-hitting
essays on gay life; writing; art.   ISBN 0-930044-57-6   7.95

AMATEUR CITY by Katherine V. Forrest. 224 pp. A Kate
Delafield mystery. First in a series.   ISBN 0-930044-55-X   10.95

THE SOPHIE HOROWITZ STORY by Sarah Schulman. 176 pp.
Engaging novel of madcap intrigue.   ISBN 0-930044-54-1   7.95

THE YOUNG IN ONE ANOTHER'S ARMS by Jane Rule.
224 pp. Classic Jane Rule.   ISBN 0-930044-53-3   9.95

OLD DYKE TALES by Lee Lynch. 224 pp. Extraordinary stories
of our diverse Lesbian lives.   ISBN 0-930044-51-7   8.95

AGAINST THE SEASON by Jane Rule. 224 pp. Luminous,
complex novel of interrelationships.   ISBN 0-930044-48-7   8.95

LOVERS IN THE PRESENT AFTERNOON by Kathleen Fleming.
288 pp. A novel about recovery and growth.   ISBN 0-930044-46-0   8.95

TOOTHPICK HOUSE by Lee Lynch. 264 pp. Love between two
Lesbians of different classes.   ISBN 0-930044-45-2   7.95

CONTRACT WITH THE WORLD by Jane Rule. 340 pp. Power-
ful, panoramic novel of gay life.   ISBN 0-930044-28-2   9.95

THIS IS NOT FOR YOU by Jane Rule. 284 pp. A letter to a
beloved is also an intricate novel.   ISBN 0-930044-25-8   8.95

OUTLANDER by Jane Rule. 207 pp. Short stories and essays by
one of our finest writers.   ISBN 0-930044-17-7   8.95

ODD GIRL OUT by Ann Bannon.   ISBN 0-930044-83-5   5.95
I AM A WOMAN 84-3; WOMEN IN THE SHADOWS 85-1;   each
JOURNEY TO A WOMAN 86-X; BEEBO BRINKER 87-8. Golden
oldies about life in Greenwich Village.

JOURNEY TO FULFILLMENT, A WORLD WITHOUT MEN, and   3.95
RETURN TO LESBOS. All by Valerie Taylor   each

These are just a few of the many Naiad Press titles — we are the oldest and
largest lesbian/feminist publishing company in the world. Please request a
complete catalog. We offer personal service; we encourage and welcome
direct mail orders from individuals who have limited access to bookstores
carrying our publications.